PENGUI[illegible]

SOMETHING I NEVER TOLD YOU

Shravya loves to find hidden stories around her and write novels about them. Formerly a corporate employee, she managed to flee the madness after a few years of boredom to become a full-time writer. She is a sucker for romance and strives to pen down exciting stories. When she is not reading and writing, she is out enjoying nature, playing with her dogs or cooking for her family.

She lives in Melbourne with her family, in a house with a barren backyard and a lifetime's collection of books.

SHRAVYA BHINDER

Something I Never Told You

An imprint of Penguin Random House

PENGUIN METRO READS

USA | Canada | UK | Ireland | Australia
New Zealand | India | South Africa | China

Penguin Metro Reads is part of the Penguin Random House group of companies whose addresses can be found at global.penguinrandomhouse.com

Published by Penguin Random House India Pvt. Ltd
4th Floor, Capital Tower 1, MG Road,
Gurugram 122 002, Haryana, India

Published in Penguin Metro Reads by Penguin Random House India 2019

21 20

ISBN 9780143445906

Typeset in Bembo by Manipal Digital Systems, Manipal
Printed at Thomson Press India Ltd, New Delhi

www.penguin.co.in

To life, love and everything magical!

PROLOGUE

It is 3 a.m. I am wide awake, staring at my computer screen with my palms resting on the keyboard. Earlier that evening, I had finally made a resolution and decided to act on it the very next day. But after tossing and turning in my lonely bed for a couple of hours, I chose to start writing this book right away.

Now I am sitting at my desk next to my bed, and I am trying hard to think of the point where it all began. When I was not thinking of writing the book, this story was all that I could think of, all that I could imagine and dream about. And now it is all gone as if those memories never existed, as if all of it had never happened. With a blank mind, I hear the only noise in the room: the sound of stillness.

My first task is to try and put my finger on the starting point of our story. After spending more than a few hours and struggling to determine the beginning—the time when it all started—it struck me. There never was a starting point after all!

Slowly, I begin to type, and gradually my speed picks up. I have only one purpose; that is, to be able to do justice to our love story which, like most love stories, is woven beautifully with delicate threads of love, desire, intimacy, fear, possessiveness, assurance, longing and unexpected events.

So I begin . . .

THE PRESENT

Sometimes I still find the odd strand of your hair in my room, but more often clinging to my clothes as a reminder of our time together. The earring that you had lost one rainy night after it was entangled in the button of my shirt, I found it yesterday under my bed, a little twisted because of all the force you had put in trying to get away from me, in vain. The pair of white teddy bears that you had got for me after our last fight still sits on my study table, blaming me for what I had done. Almost every day I find these memories of yours, lost in my room, scattered around me like a web that won't let me come out of the past. Not that I want to, I am happier living caved under these beautiful memories than face the ugly present.

These random things that I find everywhere transport me back into our once beautiful and perfect world—the world before we started fighting, the world before I started ignoring you, the world before I stopped saying, 'I love you', the world before ego crawled between us, and our world before last August.

Now that you are gone, on lonely nights I play your favourite songs—old Bollywood numbers. These songs remind me of your glowing face, and that pure, playful and infectious smile of yours that I miss the most. I sit all night and listen to those songs, staring at the empty walls in my bedroom which were once filled with your pictures. Sometimes, I walk up to the window to witness the busy lives of people who are lucky to be with people they love. The winds which once played with your beautiful hair, turn their back on me in disappointment every time they find me standing alone at the window, preoccupied with gloom.

Ever since I have come back to Delhi, I wake up in the middle of the night bathed in my sweat, curled up on the bed, alone and shivering. The bed still smells of you, of the time when you were with me, and I feel safe, enveloped in your fragrance. It reminds me of the dreams we shared together and numerous plans we wove under the stars; the warmth of nights we spent sleeping intertwined in one another, and the nights that we didn't sleep a wink. Memories of you calm me down and comfort me, but not for long. As soon as I shut my eyes, an unknown force drags me mercilessly into the same nightmares. I relive the horrors again multiple times every single night. I am not complaining about the dreams, for I am the reason why things happened the way they did. I do not mind the suffering, but I cannot bear to see your hollow, empty eyes that look through me. People have been telling me that I do not exist for you any more, but I am not ready to let go; not yet. Because you are still the pivot of my world, and I cannot bear the thought that I do not even exist in yours.

Since you left, I have learnt a lot about life and love. Nothing is permanent; time changes, and it changes everything around us—sometimes for the better and sometimes for the worse—and no one can do anything about it. No matter how much we think we control our own lives and those of others around us, the fact is that we are not at all in control of anything. Without you, nothing is the same. Reminiscing hurts me but I need to hold on to these little echoes from the past, or I will go mad with your sudden absence. I never imagined my life without you, and I cannot go back into that reality just yet.

I have learnt only one thing in my life—that we should not stop expressing our love, ever!

After some time together, we usually stop telling our beloveds how much they mean to us. We stop saying, 'I love you', and start taking each other for granted. The comfort of company creeps in. In our last few days together, I had entirely stopped putting in an effort into our relationship. I took you for granted, I took what was between us for granted as I never knew that all could be lost in the blink of an eye. The few times when I did tell you how much I loved you, I failed to stand by it. I should have told you more often how much you mean to me; I should have not hesitated in saying the three most significant yet sparingly used words in most modern relationships. I never thought that you could go anywhere, that I could lose you. Destiny tricked me and shook my world. When in love, we should tell our beloved how we feel about them; every day, every hour if we can, every minute if we must. Sadly, I realize that you are not there with me so I can rectify my mistakes. I acted like a fool.

Life is moving forward for everybody around me, but I am exactly where you left me, for I do not want to move on without you. Days are passing at their usual pace, but I have no recollection of any instances now, for it feels as if I am stuck in a time machine. Every time I think of you, I close my eyes and go back in time to the last time I held your delicate hands in mine and tried to search through your eyes to find a way to your soul. All I remember is you—us—and my mistakes. I should have stopped you; I should have let you talk, I should have listened to you. Yesterday, in your eyes I saw nothing. There was nothing in them for me, neither love nor hatred, neither ridicule nor anger.

The image of your face haunts every waking moment of my life. When I look into the mirror each morning, I hate the person who stares back at me. Not for what he did but for what he didn't do when he had the chance. I think just like you, I too am damaged beyond repair.

I pray to God for mercy and wish there was a way to turn back the clock and go back in time. I pray for another chance to relive that fateful night. I want to go back in time and tell you how much you mean to me, how ardently I have loved you all my life and always will. How I wish the walls of my ego had crumbled that night and been buried under the immense love I have always felt for you. How I wish I had disobeyed the devil in me, when I planned to make you suffer remorse for one more night. How I wish I had let you finish what you wanted to say and sealed my lips with yours. I want to go back in time and embrace you, and never let you go. I should have brought you back home with me. I wish that night would come back and give me another chance to make it all right, to hold you tight and to change our destiny.

When I come home from work, I miss hearing you humming as you unlock the door for me. I miss the coy smile which was reserved only for me. Instead of your beautiful presence, I am now welcomed home by emptiness and a house full of memories of you. Your mother took away all your pictures. I begged her not to, but she thought it was for good for both of us. My room is nothing but blank white walls now, and these empty walls start closing in on me as soon as they find me drifting back in memories and thinking about you. My loneliness engulfs me, and the demons take me with them into nightmares. I wish you could come back to me, talk to me, tell me how your day has been and ask me about mine. I want to hear you tell me how much you missed me all day; I wish to kiss your forehead once again. I would do anything to listen to you laugh once again.

I want life to give me another chance to know more about you, your dreams, your aspirations and ambitions, your opinion on things that matter to you and also on the ones that don't. I know I have made many mistakes, hurt you many times, broken your heart and been mean, but I beg for your forgiveness like I never have. I want you to tell me once that you still love me and do not think that I am the monster I think I am.

As I write this, I know that nothing that I wish for can come true, but I will wait for a miracle to happen. I will wait for you to come back to me, and for us to start our lives from where we left off. I will wait for you to love me back again, even if it means waiting till eternity.

NIRMAN VIHAR METRO STATION, NEW DELHI

AUGUST 2017

'Why thirty? We agreed on twenty-five before I sat in your auto. I pay only Rs 20 every day. I can pay Rs 5 extra, that too because I am running late for work. That is all I have,' I almost screamed at the auto wallah who was in no mood to leave the golden opportunity of further spoiling my already spoilt morning. He seemed to have sensed that I was late for something. He asked me for Rs 25 instead of the usual twenty, and when I paid him the same at the end of my ride, he asked for more.

'There was so much traffic, bhaiya ji,' his response was quick and well-rehearsed. He smiled at me, putting all his teeth and part of his gums on display. I assumed that the motive behind this act was to earn some extra bucks early in the morning. If he cared for my opinion, I would have advised him not to open his mouth in a way that showed his tobacco-stained teeth, in public places or he could be jailed for terrorizing people with his fangs. His teeth were definitely more than the required number, packed and clustered in his regular-size jaw, overlapping each other. I quickly took my eyes off his mouth to stop the uncalled-for scrutiny and started searching my pockets to see if I had any more cash on me.

I was running very late for work that day, which was also my first day of working with my new manager. I wondered if I was going to be able to retain my job after creating such a bad impression with my delayed entry at the office. It was an open secret that my new manager was a strict guy. He loved taking disciplinary actions so much that they could even be described as his work hobby. I feared that I would be kicked out of my job, without much discussion, only a few days before I had a chance to use my newly delivered debit card for the first time. Surviving in a consulting firm was tough for a fresher, tougher if you knew nothing and were always late. I belonged to the second category of course. My name is Ronnie D., and I am not a musician; though I wished to be one when I was five years old.

Well, actually, my name is Raunak Dhodi. After years of being teased because of my traditional-sounding name, I changed it to Ronnie during college because I wanted to make friends and appear cool. Honestly, neither of the two happened. In fact, most of my life I have had only two very good friends. Both of them are the people I have spent most of my life with—my cousins. But I shall talk about them later.

So, I searched frantically and found not a single penny in the back pockets of my trousers, and it turned out that the front pockets were not a penny richer than their counterparts either. However, I did manage to scoop out two Rs 2 coins from the secret pocket in my wallet, the pocket which was really a hole between the lining and the outside flap. This made it Rs 4. One more was needed. Hoping to find at least a lone rupee coin hiding somewhere in my bag, I unzipped it to put my poverty on display right outside the metro station. Other than my laptop and metro card, there was little else I could find.

'I do not have more money,' I told the auto driver one last time, straightening my shoulders.

He looked at my palm with the two shiny coins in it. 'Then I will take Rs 4 more,' he declared shamelessly. With no other option in sight, I handed over my only assets to him to get him off my back.

'This day is the worst day in the history of all the bad days I have had in my life,' I mumbled to myself, climbing up the deserted stairs. No, the metro station was not deserted, it was full of commuters just like any other day, but most commuters preferred the escalators over the stairs. Hence, I was amongst the few climbing up the stairs. I reached the automated doors at the entry, and put my hand in my pocket to pull out my metro card. Nothing. *Where is it?* I wondered, and panicking I frantically searched in my bag, then my back pockets, front pockets, and even the shirt pocket where I never put anything. It was not on me. Where was it? I remembered seeing it a little while ago and thought hard to remember where it could be.

'Shit!' I exclaimed, trying to recall the last time I'd seen it. Then I remembered that I had seen it outside the station when I'd opened my bag for the wretched auto wallah. 'It must have fallen out of my bag then. I will never find it now,' I despaired, and dashed down the stairs. Dropping something in Delhi and hoping to find it seconds later is too much wishful thinking. I'd lost the card loaded with

Rs 130.75. If I ever caught even a glimpse of it in my lifetime, it would be a miracle.

Worried and scared, I frantically searched for the card on the stairs and then on the footpath. It was nowhere to be seen.

'Shit, shit, shit!' I knew saying it thrice made nothing right, yet three times the usual shit was the only way to describe my situation at that point—stuck outside a metro station, penniless and late for work.

I turned around, contemplating a walk back home. It was going to be a very time-consuming and tiring affair, but as they say—desperate times need desperate measures. I live close to 3 km away from the metro station, and I am not an athlete, nor was I back then. But a poor man should walk, I told myself, and looked back at the stairs with a small ray of hope still flickering in my heart.

The deserted stairs were not deserted any more; a girl sat on the second step with her head bowed down. She was talking to someone over the phone. Her lovely long hair fell over her delicate shoulders, and I was unable to see her face which was buried under her lustrous hair. I was standing only four or five steps away from her, and I noticed that she had rings on almost all her fingers and I recognized one of them—the gold ring on her index finger with a green sapphire in it. Her fair, delicate hands were busy untangling imaginary knots in her shiny hair. Dressed in a white kurta and salwar, she was lost in her conversation, unaware and unfazed that her blue dupatta, beautifully spread on the last stair, was sweeping the dusty path to the stairs. I was going to be late for work and was most definitely going to lose my job, but I froze when I saw her. Her hair, her posture, the way her hands moved, made me skip more than a few heartbeats. I knew her. Unintentionally, my eyes wandered over her sheer dupatta through which her feet in golden *juttis* (footwear) were visible.

In my head, a Shahrukh Khan song was about to be played in the background, and I was inches away from drifting into a dream song and bursting into a dance sequence when suddenly I spotted it, under her dupatta—my metro card! Well, it was a metro card and could have been mine or someone else's. But as long as it had enough money on it to take me to my destination, I did not care whose card it was. 'Excuse me,' I said, walking towards the girl who sat there like she owned the station. She raised her head. Her dark-brown hair half covered her face. She transferred her mobile phone to her left hand and gently swept away her mane from her face with her fingers. Our eyes met, and within a flash of a moment it was 2015 again.

'Adira?' her name fell out of my mouth abruptly, and she looked at me as if I were a psychopathic stalker.

EAST OF KAILASH, NEW DELHI

JUNE 2015

'I do not know, yaar. It has been three days already, and I have not made any friends,' I told my chuddi buddy, Rohit Nagpal. We were also distant cousins. He was the first of the two best friends that I had mentioned earlier. He was preparing to get into the Merchant Navy then and had taken one year off after college to make it happen. He left his dreams of joining the Merchant Navy after meeting his then girlfriend, now wife—Sagarika—and ended up owning one of the most profitable start-ups in Delhi, which is a different story altogether.

When his dad advised him to take one year off from his formal studies and prepare for the entrance exams, he decided to give it a try. It was too good an offer to decline. I wondered why my dad did not give me such offers. Taking a break and studying for a few hours a day was so much better than trying to make friends at a new college who would help me pass my exams and put in proxy attendance on my behalf.

'Why can't I join the same MBA college as my other friends from school!' I had dared to put up a brave fight before giving in to my parents' pressure. My dad had looked at me through his glasses.

'Because I do not want you to. No good will come from doing an MBA from a university in Noida. No one will give you a job. There are so many students who waste money in such colleges. Do you know what are the yearly fees of the third-rate college you want to attend? I cannot afford it, and why should I? Money does not grow on trees. I will see what college you send your kids to. Children nowadays do not value money . . .' the dreaded lecture began, ending my dreams of studying with my old friends for a few more years before adult life stung all of us.

'Your name is hilarious. Change it or else you will have no friends. These Hindu wallahs want cool friends. So be a cool dude,' Rohit had suggested mockingly, and I snapped back into reality. I saw Rohit roll off the single bed to land on the floor laughing. Once he was done with his drama, I gave him a cold stare, and thankfully he did not bring up the delicate topic again. My parents had named me after my great-grandfather as I happened to share my birthday with him. I had studied all my life in the same school, with almost the same set of people who were used to calling me 'Ronnie'.

The topic of changing my name was a delicate one, and I knew it quite well, so with my head hanging down, and my face buried in my book, I silently heard the entire class giggle every time my name was called out. It was to be my tenth day with a different set of people in my class at college. Thankfully, that day my nani (maternal grandmother) needed a hand with some cleaning at her house and I got a chance to skip college. I was glad that she asked me to help her with whatever it was and hoped that someone else got the chance to be the butt of all their jokes in my absence at college.

My nani lives in East of Kailash, a posh colony in South Delhi. After my nana's death, Nani started sharing her house and loneliness with paying guests (PGs). She used to keep only one PG in her home at a time, usually girls who were in the city to study or work. With seven boys in the family, Nani knew how much trouble a college-going guy can bring and wanted to stay away from it. Her last PG had left a few months ago to get married, and a replacement was to arrive in a few hours' time. A week ago, when Nani had told us that the new PG was a first-year student as well, both Rohit and I were delighted beyond words.

'I hope she is pretty,' Rohit chirped in while placing a sheet of newspaper in the wardrobe to line the shelves. Every time a new PG came, Nani told us to clean the closets and replace the newspaper linings in them.

'Same here,' I absent-mindedly told him, folding a colourful Sunday issue to line the topmost shelf. I am five feet eleven inches tall, and Rohit is five-four, so the top two shelves were mine while the rest of the wardrobe was his to tidy up.

'Why do you care?' he asked me wide-eyed. I wondered what he meant and looked at him for an explanation. 'Come on! You also know that you will not even look at her properly, let alone talk to her or do anything beyond that. You are too shy,' he was pulling my leg again. I wanted to give an appropriate response, but quick, witty replies are not my speciality. I avoided eye contact with Rohit and admired my handiwork instead. My part of the cleaning was done, and the top shelves of the wardrobe looked neat.

While Rohit was still busy with his part of the cleaning, I decided to laze on the bed in the cool room until Nani called us downstairs to help the new PG with her luggage. Judging from the past, they came with hardly anything more than a duffel bag and a suitcase.

Ten minutes later, exactly when Rohit closed the doors of the wooden wardrobe, we heard Nani's shrill voice from the ground floor, 'Come and help her with her bags, you two. She is here.' My nani was gifted with two separate sets of voices; one was the harsh voice which we usually heard around us, and the second was a soft, melodious voice which could put a cuckoo to shame. She used her cuckoo voice to communicate with people of high authority or our NRI relatives and their kids, and also with her PGs but only for the first few days of their stay in her house. As we descended the stairs, we heard her talk to the new girl in her soothing voice, 'You can leave your bags outside. The boys will get them and take them upstairs to your room. You follow me inside as I need to talk to you about some formalities,' she told her PG. Rohit and I looked at each other and rolled our eyes at the extra sweetness in Nani's tone.

We headed straight outside the main door where a green and yellow CNG auto was parked. I looked at the bags on the ground: two stroller bags and one duffel bag, along with one large backpack inside the auto. Rohit picked up the large backpack, and his expressions told me that he could not manage to even think of picking up anything else, so I passed him the smaller of the two stroller bags instead. I placed the duffel bag on the bigger stroller and turned around to follow Rohit upstairs.

'Bhaiya, give me Rs 50 so that I can go,' the auto wallah called after me.

'What? Rs 50? The madam didn't pay you?' I asked him, surprised.

'She was too busy on her phone, and then the Amma Ji took her in. She forgot to pay me. She did not even take her bags from the auto,' he replied with a displeased look on his face and resumed smoking his beedi. I signalled him to wait, and instead of going to the first floor with the luggage, I walked into Nani's drawing room.

Nani was nowhere to be seen. On the black leather sofa, I saw a slim figure sitting in a relaxed pose. She was dressed in a pair of denim shorts and a short-sleeved red T-shirt. Looking at her choice of dress, one could predict that Nani and she would not be friends for long. Nani had a conservative thought process when it came to the clothing her PGs should wear in the house. I looked at her again. She was sitting with her long, slim legs crossed, the left on top of the right, and she moved her left leg rhythmically while looking at the screen of her phone in her right hand. There was a delicate gold ring on her index finger with a green sapphire in it.

As I walked closer to her, she felt my presence and looked up at me. This was the first time I saw her face which became embossed on my heart forever. She had the sweetest face I had ever seen. Her skin was clear and shining, her cheeks were pink, probably due to the heat she had travelled in. Tiny sweat beads rested on her forehead; she had large almond-shaped eyes, deep and soulful. They looked through me, or that was how it felt. Her small nose and pink lips looked as if they were created by an artist in a painting. She got up from the sofa and stood to face me. Her face had a warm familiarity to it; her expressions were soft and delicate. I felt a sudden wave of nervousness rise through me, originating from my gut.

Despite remembering every minute detail of our first meeting, I hoped that she'd forget the moment when she first saw me—nothing but a creep dressed in shabby clothes and sweating like a pig. Sadly, she recalled it and bought it up in a conversation months later. I had no other option at that moment but to be honest and tell her why I behaved the way I did. It was because I felt as if I were under her spell. I distinctly remember that my eyes didn't even blink while we looked at each other. But I soon came out of that state as Nani mercilessly dragged me out of the golden haze. She walked in, making as much noise as she could with her rubber slippers slapping on her heels and gold bangles. 'Adira!' she called her.

Adira . . . her name echoed in my head. I loved the sound of it. Her name had a magical quality to it. Adira hurriedly took her eyes off me and turned them towards Nani. I tried to do the same, but my eyes wanted to stare at her more and refused to turn away. *Look elsewhere, you stupid idiot, or she will think that you have some problem with your eyes or worse, with your brains!* I told myself, but my eyes just did not cooperate. I stood there, dumbfounded, staring at Adira while Nani began chatting with her new PG. I probably even had my mouth open at the time—I do not remember as I was too engrossed in being as crazy as one could possibly be to notice such little details that made me look like an utter fool.

For the next few minutes, I heard them talk to each other, but their conversation did not register in my head. I was busy carefully noting the particulars of Adira's face: the way her lips moved as she spoke, the way she played with her hair continuously and the frown which appeared on her forehead quite frequently. She smiled at Nani, and

I looked in wonder at her beautiful lips and perfect teeth, which, mind you, were the whitest I had ever seen. Little did I know then that hers was a face that was going to keep me awake for many years to come.

Feeling my gaze, Adira turned towards me. She did not look pleased. *Just ask her about the auto fare and leave*, I heard the voice in my head trying to give me sensible advice again, but my body did not comply. Narrowing her big, brown eyes, with her hands on her tiny waist, Adira was now staring angrily at me.

NIRMAN VIHAR METRO STATION

2017

Her eyes were still the same, and so was her expression. Narrowing her big, brown eyes, Adira stared back at me. A small frown appeared on her forehead, and I came crashing back to reality from the world of memories.

Ask her to move away as your metro card is lying under her dupatta, the sensible part of my brain suggested, but as always, my eyes refused to budge, and my mouth would not open to utter even a single sound, let alone words.

She tilted her head a little towards the left and raised her hand to check her watch, indicating that she was running late for something too. Finally, I gathered some willpower and pointed towards her dupatta, trying to recover my voice and find some words. It had only been three months, but it felt as if it was ages ago when I last saw her exquisite face. Adira had left Nani's place as soon as she finished college.

'Her dad has bought her a flat somewhere in Mayur Vihar.' This was the last piece of information Rohit gave me about her two months ago.

Finally, after much struggling, my vocal cords decided to work. *Phew!* my mind said, and then bit its tongue. 'Hehehe,' an awkward, funny giggle escaped from my mouth. *Where had that come from?* I wondered, and quickly tried to do some damage control by uttering the word 'Card' very meekly.

'Card? What card?' she asked, looking every bit the annoyed diva that she was.

I decided not to say anything more at that moment. *Not your day, Ronnie.* I pointed towards her dupatta again, and her eyes followed my finger. She looked down at her dupatta and then back at me again. *Does she not remember me? It has just been three months!*

'Hold on, yaar, there is . . .' she paused and looked at me from top to toe before addressing me, 'What is it, Raunak?' *She remembers me!* I lost my voice once more, this time in excitement. 'Let me call you back once I get into the metro,' she told the person on the other end of the phone. I was looking at her after precisely three months and knew nothing about her present circumstances, yet I hoped that she was talking to a girl and not a boy.

This is your chance, Ronnie, to make a new start with her. You just have to confidently ask her to let you pick up that metro card from under her dupatta. She will be so sorry when she realizes that she wasted your time, and then maybe you guys can start talking, be friends.

Status Check: air castle building, work in progress.

'Just . . . Just my card,' I said once again.

'Oh, okay,' she said, looking cluelessly in the direction of her dupatta again. *Ask her out for a coffee. A date? No, that would be a little too desperate. Or maybe just take her number today*—I was still contemplating.

Before I could think of how to ask her out, or maybe strike up a conversation, my happy plans came under a bus called reality, because she had already turned her back on me and was walking up the stairs. The blue plastic card lay at the bottom of the stairs silently witnessing my misery. I picked it up hastily and followed Adira inside the metro station.

Our accidental encounter set off a series of flashbacks in my head, running on a loop. I recalled each and every thing as if it happened just yesterday. I followed her inside and spotted her walking towards the booth for security checks. There was a long queue at the men's security check booth, while only two other females stood in line ahead of Adira. She was done with the frisking within moments, while I stood sandwiched between other stinking men waiting for my turn; not taking my eyes off her. I saw her walk towards the entry door, swipe her metro card and then make a phone call as soon as she was inside. She did not appear to be in a hurry to board the train, and at that point relief ran over me.

Finally, it was my turn to be checked by a middle-aged policeman who looked bored of his job. I stood on the podium with my arms stretched out. He ran a metal detector all over my body and then let me pass. I picked up my laptop from the stack of bags on the X-ray machine and dashed towards the entry door. *Please, God, please make this card have enough money to take me inside*, I prayed hard, and to my surprise, my prayers were answered. Turns out that it was indeed my card!

Once inside the metro station, I took slow steps and crossed her without looking at her. As I went past her, I inhaled deeply a sweet fragrance enveloping her. She smelled like a cocktail of scents—a blend of her shampoo, a purple mist, and her favourite body wash from the Body Shop—British Rose. How do I know all this? Well, I had gone shopping with her many times during the last three years. Not precisely with her though; she used to go shopping with her friend—Tamanna—every other weekend, and I used to drag Rohit to the same places. Stalking? No, it was more like birdwatching for Rohit and a one-sided date for me.

I took the escalators for my metro towards Connaught Place, hoping that she would do the same. The opposite platform was where the train for Vaishali arrived. While I took my place on the icy-cold bench of the platform, I calculated that even if she boarded the train for Vaishali, I would be able to see her one more time. I secretly wished she would come to the same platform though.

One after the other, five metro trains halted and left for Connaught Place. I was no longer worried about being late for my job, because I was sure that by now my manager must have typed my termination letter and I had no job. I was only going to be late to collect my termination letter for skipping work without informing anyone. *It is okay; it is just a job*, I told my troubled mind, which was already thinking of the consequences my foolishness would bring my way. *Nothing is more important than my love of two years—one-sided love of two years*—I corrected my own statement, and that was when the worries started making sense.

I decided to get on the next train and go to the office. The clock on the platform showed it would be arriving in another two minutes. *Two minutes—she can still come to the platform at any moment*, I thought, and hoped she would board the same train as me. The train decided to surprise the clock and me and arrived one minute earlier than expected. I looked at my phone to distract myself from the disappointment. No missed call or messages from anyone, not even from work.

The doors opened, and I squeezed myself in along with many others. Miraculously, I managed to get a seat right next to the door since I happened to be there as a person was getting off. I parked myself like a rock there. The announcement for the closing of the doors played inside the train, and I turned my head to look out for her one last time.

I blinked my eyes in disbelief as I saw Adira running towards the train I was in. She was holding a girl's hand whose face was hidden underneath a printed cotton dupatta. They rushed into the ladies' compartment just before the doors closed, and we began our journey. The train moved slowly and then picked up speed, matching my heartbeats. I got up from my seat. Anyone who has travelled in the Delhi metro during peak hours knows the level of sacrifice that I made that day; it is the most significant thing a metro traveller can ever do for anyone. I found myself making my way to the compartment next to the one where Adira was.

It didn't take me long to find her in the maddening crowd. Her back was towards me—the beautiful 'Om' tattoo at the nape of her neck peeped out from the translucent cloth of her kurta. She had secured a few loose strands of hair behind her ear and was talking to the other girl, moving her hands and head animatedly. Leaning against a pole, I smiled like an idiot—running back and forth in time. I resolved to get off at the same station as her and talk to her, finally!

The train crossed station after station and reached Rajiv Chowk. I was supposed to get down there, and I did because Adira and her friend got down at the same location. I hoped that her friend would leave her there so that I could talk to her, but I guess that was too much to expect. Another idea came crashing down when her friend took off that hideous, cloth from her face which she must have used as a shield against the pollution in Delhi. It was Tamanna!

TAMANNA

Ever since Adira had arrived at my nani's house, my visits there had dramatically increased. Earlier, when Nani used to look for a volunteer to do her household chores or pay some bills or bathe Samba, her furry pug, Rohit, Piyush and I vanished from the scene, and if caught by Nani, we made as many lame excuses as we could think of to get her off our backs. But since her new PG had arrived, both Piyush and I were at Nani's beck and call. In fact, I wondered if Piyush had stopped attending his classes altogether just to be in the house when Adira walked in and out for college. And the last thing I had heard from Rohit was that Piyush had even managed to take Adira's mobile number. The rascal, who was also related to me, my maternal cousin was planning to take Adira out for shopping to Khan Market the coming Saturday.

'You would just keep buying tinda (gourds) for Nani, and Piyush will marry this girl one day,' Rohit said abruptly one day on our way to the vegetable market. Nani had asked us to get 1 kg of tinda (gourds). Rohit was not keen on impressing Adira, but he was still there whenever Nani called him. I wondered why but never dared to ask him as he had the tendency to get upset very quickly. That day, when he passed that uncalled-for comment, I felt like punching him hard, but deciding where to hit him to hurt him the most took me forever, and my anger cooled down. Just like witty responses, quick physical reactions are also not my thing.

Honestly, when I think of it, he was not entirely wrong when he made that comment. Piyush had seen Adira precisely a week after I had. He was visiting Nani the following Saturday when they bumped into each other on the stairs, and he did what he does best at the sight of a girl. He drooled over her just the way Samba drools over a boiled egg, and within minutes Piyush declared that he had fallen hopelessly in love with Adira. He confided in Rohit, and as expected, Rohit kept me informed about all the devilish plans Piyush was making to woo her. He was the closest to being anything related to the word 'charming' out of all the men in our family, and if anyone had a chance to woo her, it had to be him and no one else. I wanted to be him: easy and fun-loving, motivated no matter how the day was, but I failed miserably in all the good departments and was scared of losing Adira to him long before I even got a chance to know her last name. Her last name is Kapoor, by the way.

It was the second Sunday since the girl had invaded my dreams, and Piyush was already ahead of me. 'Do you also have her number?' I asked Rohit, sulking.

'I can get it for you,' he replied as clearly as is possible with an entire samosa stuffed into his mouth. We had come back from the market, and Nani had gone out to meet some relative. Nani was not at home, but samosas were, and Rohit did not want them to feel lonely. So, he gave them the company of chow mien which he had stuffed into his tummy while I decided which tinda looked and felt the freshest. That evening Adira was not home either. Her school friend was to arrive from Pune that morning and, surprisingly, Nani had given her permission to share her bedroom with her friend, provided this friend of hers paid some money for her share of household expenses like food and electricity, etc. Piyush had gone with her to the airport to pick her friend up—bastard!

At 4 p.m., a taxi stopped in front of the main door. I peeped through the curtains and saw Adira get down with her friend—a thin, dusky female with short, bouncy hair and way too many piercings to count all across her earlobe. She had a bright smile, and she appeared to be someone who could laugh easily and cried rarely. Following them, Piyush also stepped out of the taxi and paid the driver.

They did not take long to come into the house in the same order.

'Come, Tamanna. Let me show you our room!' excitedly, Adira took her friend into her room without even acknowledging mine or Rohit's presence in the hallway. Once they left, both Rohit and I looked at Piyush to find him staring in a disgusting way at the girls with his mouth wide open.

'Stop ogling!' I scolded him angrily, as frustration was building up in me by the minute, and his lewd acts were not helping.

'I am in love!' he declared, still looking in the direction where the girls had stood, as if he were dreaming.

'Shut up! Adira is way out of our league,' I told him, stating the obvious, which both Rohit and I could see clearly, but Piyush was not willing to accept.

Surprising both of us, Piyush said, 'I am talking about Tamanna.'

It took him just one week to ask her out and three to start dating her. If you ask me my opinion, even Tamanna was out of his league, but it seems that no one is ever interested in asking me anything.

Many years later, I asked him if he remembered the exact moment when he knew he was in love with Tamanna. I still remember what he said and knew instantly that it was for real. 'Well, it was the first time when I gazed into her dark eyes. That was the moment when I knew that my soul had finally found the place it needed to rest in. Love penetrates the hardest of hearts in the blink of an eye.' That was also the evening when Gulzar Sahab found a new fan.

RAJIV CHOWK METRO STATION

2017

Tamanna was Piyush's fiancée by then, and they were to be married soon. Piyush was in the US for business studies, and Tamanna had recently started working full-time. Since she and I had met many times, she knew me too. Somehow, I had a feeling that she even knew about my crush on Adira, thanks to Piyush. But being the lovely girl she is, she never brought the topic up in our conversations. She was my family, and I did not want to be caught in an awkward moment in front of her or Adira. There was only one thing I could do—*Mission Abort!* I told the bouncy feeling in my heart, and it left me instantly. I quietly stepped into the next metro towards Gurgaon.

I got down at the metro station, which was close to my office, and took the office shuttle—a free bus service provided to all employees every half an hour. I dashed into the building as soon as the bus halted. Talking to Adira was not in my fate, but I hoped that saving my job was. Quite a few people were waiting for the elevator, so I took the stairs instead. *Ten floors—it is not a big deal for a fit young man like me!* or so I thought. The morale boost worked for the first three floors. By the time I reached the fifth floor, my tongue was hanging out of my mouth, and at the ninth floor it was sweeping the floor underneath. 'Only one more floor to go—you can do this!' I motivated myself loudly.

Just then, my phone buzzed. It was an unknown landline number from Gurgaon. 'Hello,' I answered, panting.

'Raunak Dhodi?' the male voice on the other end was stern.

'Yes, sir, who is this?'

'I am your manager, Rajbir. We are all in meeting room number five. Whenever you come to work, come in here,' he told me authoritatively.

'Yes, sir, I am almost . . .' he disconnected the call before I could make up an excuse.

'Holy shit!' I mustered all the courage and moved towards meeting room number five.

The New Manager

Five well-groomed girls and four formally dressed men sat with their heads bowed, around a wooden table in the room. The glass door was closed. A tall, lean man wearing a light-blue shirt and a pair of black trousers stood in one corner of the room. With a red marker, he was carefully writing on a whiteboard with his back towards the rest of the group as well as the door where I stood looking at them. I waited at the door, peeping in, trying to analyse the situation; he stopped writing and turned around, looking straight in the direction where I stood peeking in at the group. With his right hand, he signalled me to step into the room.

'Hello, sir, I am . . .' before I could say more, he hushed me with the look in his eyes and a finger on his lips. The group sitting at the table turned to look at me; most of them were trying to suppress their smiles.

'Hello, do we have an addition to the group?' I heard a beautiful foreign voice ask. Looking in the direction of the sound, I figured out that the team was in the middle of a call with someone.

The company I worked for had clients in the US, the UK and Australia. My new team looked after the Australian clients. 'Our team benchmarks the salaries for its employees in Australia and looks after their employee satisfaction surveys as well as data analytics,' I was told later by a colleague. When I think of it, I cannot understand how a person of average intelligence like me ended up in a niche job like this. Rather than being happy about getting into the new team, I was always scared that I was not cut out for it, and that I might not be able to perform as well as expected.

'Yes, Cathy,' the guy in the blue shirt walked up to the table and addressed the voice on the other end. 'The newest team member has joined us late, very late,' he looked at me with penetrating eyes, and I immediately felt intimidated by him.

Cathy asked me to introduce myself to her. I was not prepared for this. I am never ready for introductions. 'Hi, my name is Ronnie . . .' I began reluctantly.

'Isn't your name Raunak?' the man interjected yet again.

'Yes . . . yes, madam, My name is Raunak Dhodi, and I am new to the team,' I said sulkily and as quickly as I could. All the girls giggled but calmed down instantly as soon as the guy with the marker gave them a cold stare. I felt my ears become hot again. The unnecessary interruption from the stranger during my intro had irked me. I kept my eyes down and stared at the carpet to calm myself down. I knew my anger would do me more harm than good, and I had never harmed anyone with my anger, so it was basically a useless emotion for me.

'Do not call me madam, please. Rau . . . Raunak, is it?' Cathy asked politely.

'Yes, it is, Cathy. So, we were discussing the requirements . . .' the man was getting on my nerves by answering all the questions in my place. He signalled me to take the lone empty seat. I walked towards it slowly and sank into the chair as low as I could, wishing to be invisible to the world.

'Why do you not change your name to Ronnie officially?' Rohit had once again suggested a week ago. Damn it! If only I would've acted on his advice for once, and done something about this name.

Fifteen minutes later, Cathy and most of my new team members were still discussing the requirements for some project.

'Cathy, I have a suggestion to make here . . .' the man in the blue shirt continued his conversation with Cathy, and my mind drifted into a sea of memories.

'. . . Raunak should try it. What do you say? It will help him to understand the process and get absorbed into the system.' These words brought me back to the meeting room, and the transition was not as smooth as I would have wanted it to be.

What? What should Raunak try? Why is he saying my name? Shit!

I looked at the man saying this with a questioning expression. I had no clue what was happening at the meeting. Frantically, I looked at the whiteboard. Some words were scribbled on it—charts, comparative analysis, data by Thursday—a better plan. *What has this bugger signed me up for?*

'Yes, of course, Rajbir, we can do that. What do you think, Raunak? Will you be able to manage it?' Cathy asked me.

So this is Rajbir? His interjections suddenly made sense, and I inspected the devil of a person who stood in front of me with his hands resting on his waist. I'd expected someone more mature, older maybe—like our college professor—to be my manager. He looked so young, and I wondered how I would manage to take orders from him.

'Yes, madam . . . oh, Cathy . . . sorry,' the group laughed again.

'He says he will be happy to do it, Cathy!' for the first time since I had stepped into the room, Rajbir's interjection sounded like music to my ears. I listened to the rest of the call very attentively and pretended to take notes, not that it helped as I understood nothing. It had already been too late.

The meeting ended at 1.15 p.m. One after the other, the entire team left the room. It was only Rajbir and me who stayed back.

He said he wanted to talk to me since I had already defaulted on punctuality earlier in that morning and my performance at the meeting made my case worse. I was a bit scared, but there was nothing I could do. For the first time, he asked me something about me—my expectations from him—to be specific. Since I had nothing specific in my mind, I let him take the lead. Rajbir listed his expectations of me as a team member—the first being punctuality.

Later, he opened a big Excel sheet with lots and lots of data on it. I was sitting across from him, so he kept rotating the laptop every once in a while for me to be able to see the screen. Whatever he said for the next many minutes, went straight over my head, and I could not catch a thing. 'Move over and sit next to me so that you can see the screen. I will help you get your laptop as soon as we are done with this,' he told me, as if he were reading my mind.

'Of course!' I said enthusiastically, and pulled the chair next to him.

Meeting room number five was located at the centre of the tenth floor. All around the room were workstations. Next to the meeting room, was a pantry area with a couple of table and chairs.

Both of us were sitting facing the pantry door. I looked towards the bright laptop screen. Before he could begin again, there was a sudden commotion outside the pantry gate, and I looked in that direction to see what it was.

It was someone's birthday. A group of people was walking into the pantry with a big box of what appeared to be a cake and a few colourful birthday caps—a newly hired training batch. It was not difficult to guess; their mood was carefree, their body language relaxed—they appeared to be the complete opposite of the kind of people who worked on the production floor.

While Rajbir crazily clicked on the folders, scanning them, I checked out the room which had nothing unusual in it—a table, a few chairs, a dustbin, some markers. 'Here, got it!' my manager exclaimed, and my dull observation ended. He rubbed his hands together in excitement, as if a genie would appear out of them, and clicked on a file named Gordon & Son's Deck.

From the corner of my eye, I could still see the unusually happy bunch going in and out of the pantry creating a ruckus. 'Okay,' he said. As soon as the Deck flashed open on the screen, precisely at that moment, I saw someone familiar at the pantry door. My gaze darted in that direction—it was her. She was standing at the door, with a little cake in her hair. She was giggling like a child; her face lit up like a thousand candles, and when she laughed, her eyes sparkled brighter than stars. She was the same as I'd remembered her to be—I felt the meeting room vanish into thin air, and the warmth of her smile and laughter filled my lungs. I inhaled deeply. Her laughter had the same effect on me that the sunlight has on trees. I felt alive when she smiled. Just like that, my day was brighter than any other day at work because the unexpected had happened—Adira Kapoor was at my office.

'The laptop has not walked out of the room yet!' Rajbir made a sarcastic remark to bring me back, and I apologetically looked at the boring screen. He started explaining something, but in my mind, I had lost track. I was now concentrating on what Adira was doing. I sneakily glanced at the door again. She was not there. Instead, some other girl stood in the same spot. But I could see her dupatta. It was the same dupatta I'd seen in the morning. *It was her!* I could not have been mistaken in identifying Adira. Maybe she works here too—my heart swelled with hopes and dreams.

Is it her birthday? No, it can't be. Her birthday is in December—14 December to be precise.

14 DECEMBER 2015

My days at the Hindu college were not going great. I only attended college for the minimum number of days that were strictly required to sit my exams. I had not made many friends, just two. We were more like weekend friends, actually, as we never met during the week at the college. In fact, that was the main reason we had become friends in the first place. As neither of us felt inclined to attend college every day, we had made a pact. I went to college on Mondays; Sanjay, the second guy in the group, went to college on Wednesdays; and Ankit, the third, did the same on Fridays. We proxied each other's attendance and made three copies of the notes for the days we attended college. On weekends, we met at a famous sweet shop for a breakfast of chole bhature, and exchanged notes. On the days when I was free, which were many of course, I preferred to go to Noida and hang out with my other friends. They too had no interest in attending their classes at their college, which made things very easy.

My Saturday afternoons, as well as Sundays, were spent at Nani's house, helping the old lady with the household chores. Adira was a student at Miranda House and was very regular at college. For the first few days after making an arrangement with my bhature friends, I strolled around Miranda House hoping to get a glimpse of her. Yes, I know this sounds very filmy and stereotyped, but when you are in love, you do not care about anything—especially if the desire is still one-sided and you only get to see the girl as you would watch a weekly soap opera star. But she never stepped out during her college hours, which is why I soon gave up that practice and went back to enjoying my days in Noida instead.

While I was at Nani's house on the weekends, I had so far exchanged only a few hellos with Adira. She had my number, and I had hers. I used to take a screenshot of each of her new DPs (display pictures) she uploaded on her WhatsApp. Then I had created a Facebook account too, just for her. I made it with a fake name and put up Justin Bieber's picture as my profile pic. I had no friends because I had not made this account to make friends with anyone new on Facebook. I just wanted to know more about Adira. I learnt a life lesson though—beautiful girls do not accept random friend requests from people claiming to be Bieber. When I sent Adira a Facebook friend request, she not only declined it but blocked the fake me as well. That was the end of my tryst with Facebook, at least for the time being.

Even though I considered FB an utter waste of time, I could not thank it enough for providing me with one useful piece of information about Adira—her birthday. It was on 14 December.

'It is today,' I told Rohit excitedly as we headed towards Nani's house.

'Why are *you* getting so excited then? Has she invited you to her party?' he asked sarcastically. I chose to ignore his comment.

'I did not even know that there is a party until you told me,' I responded in an indifferent tone.

'Then why are you so excited?' he poked my arm.

How could I tell him that I had finally found the most fantastic present for the most amazing girl I knew—not only expensive but amazing! In fact, it was so expensive I could not afford it, and I intended to borrow some money from Rohit. We were just a few steps away from Nani's house when I decided to stop beating around the bush and hit the nail directly on the head. 'I need some money,' I said.

Rohit halted.

'A loan, actually,' I added.

'Okay . . .' he looked at me as if he did not understand what I meant.

'I need the loan from you!' I said it out loud so that there was no confusion in his head.

'Let me guess. You want to buy a gift for Adira and have no money, is that it?' Rohit knew my family's financial circumstances, and I expected him to be a little nice to me when it came to money. My parents gave me only Rs 300 a week to manage my expenses, which included my transport to college, lunch, etc. I never complained about the money as I was very well aware that it was the best that they could manage. Rohit was my only hope. Then again, he might not lend me the money—this scary thought immediately crossed my mind. I had not pictured this situation and was not ready with a backup plan. Rohit had been my saviour when it came to money ever since I could recall.

'Ronnie, you have been singing non-stop for the past two months about confessing your stupid feelings to her on her birthday. How could you have not thought of saving enough money to buy her a present for her birthday!' Rohit asked irritably.

I had no answer to his question, but I was happy as we were still discussing the matter. *It is not a straight 'no' then*—I shamelessly thought. I wondered if I was supposed to answer him but decided to skip it then. Not the right time. I looked back at him with sad, imploring eyes—on purpose. They always worked with Rohit.

'Now, do not make such a sad face. How much are we talking about here?'

'Rs 2000,' I told him without meeting his eye. It was the largest amount of money I had ever borrowed from him, but without asking any more questions he handed his debit card over to me.

'I want you to accompany me to the shop so that we can buy her present. Would you like to come?' I asked him, and he readily agreed. I loved him for being the nice brother that he was.

We reached the jewellery store in Khan Market on Rohit's new black Pulsar. 'This? Seriously?' Rohit was surprised, and he managed to suppress his laughter as he parked his bike outside. I had never got a gift for a girl in my life till that day, not even for my own sister and the fact that I had decided to buy jewellery for Adira on her birthday had my cousin in stitches for at least five minutes.

As soon as we walked in, we were welcomed by an elderly gentleman sitting at the counter. As we did not appear to be serious buyers, he did not pay us much attention post the initial greeting. 'I want to buy something that I saw in the store this morning,' I told him, and watched his expression turn from indifferent to eager in a matter of seconds.

I walked farther into the store, and he followed me to the section that had delicate bracelets on display. About twenty minutes later, we left the place with a red velvet box.

'When and how are you going to give it to her?' Rohit asked me for the umpteenth time, turning his head a little as we drove back to Nani's house.

'I do not know yet,' I replied from the back seat, and started thinking of a plan.

On reaching Nani's house, we hurried into the study room on the ground floor. I had not seen Adira since the morning, and I hoped to not bump into her before I was ready with my present and a plan.

I sank into the black leather chair next to the wooden study table and started looking through the drawers trying to find a decently operational pen and some paper.

'Do you need something?' Rohit asked me just when I managed to find both things in the last drawer on the table.

'Nah,' I replied, and started recalling the words I had thought up during the ride back home to write on the note.

'I will be outside,' Rohit said, and walked out, closing the doors behind him. I knew he was giving me space and time to think.

All by myself in the study, I started to write.

Thirty minutes later, I was done writing the most beautiful thing I had written, read or heard in my entire life, until then. I hoped that the message was good enough for Adira to understand my feelings for her. As I folded the paper neatly and pasted it on top of the gift box with a strip of sticky tape, Rohit walked back in with a stupid smile on his face, indicating that he was up to something. 'I have some good news for you,' he said, rubbing his hands together and grinning mischievously.

'What are you so excited about?' I asked, placing the box carefully in the uppermost drawer.

'We are going to Adira's birthday party!' he replied excitedly.

I stared back at him in surprise, my eyes wide open. 'How on earth did you manage that?' I asked.

'Tamanna was chattily inviting Piyush to Adira's birthday party at her friend's house. As I was with him, she had to extend the invite to me as well. I am sure you know how shameless I can be when the situation demands. So, I asked her if I could bring you along. She looked at Piyush and then reluctantly said yes. I do not like this Tamanna girl . . .' I hugged him hard before he could say any more. This was just what I needed.

The party was at Malviya Nagar, a South Delhi colony. Rohit, Piyush and I reached there half an hour before the set time, as Piyush wanted to help his girlfriend with the arrangements. Rohit and I tagged along with him in his car, and we had no option but to sit there and wait for the others to arrive.

One after the other, many unknown faces walked in. Most of them were girls from Miranda House. There were a few of Tamanna's friends and relatives, and a guy named Sahil came in with a big bouquet of red roses. He was Tamanna's childhood friend's brother. He worked at a bank in Gurgaon. Rohit updated me with the details of all the men who had arrived at the party without their partners. I marvelled at how much he knew about other people. Finally, at 7 p.m. Adira graced the party with her presence, along with a small group of friends—two girls and a beefed-up boy who could have passed himself off as a gym instructor. He could not take his eyes off Adira and tried to put his paws around her at every opportunity.

'Who is this guy?' I asked Rohit.

'I don't know,' he said, shamelessly ogling a girl with long, silky hair wearing a green sweater and black skirt. Thankfully, she was busy chatting with someone on her phone and did not notice my cousin, who was already frothing at the mouth.

I chose to ignore the crowd around me, which also included both my cousins, and focused on my plan for the night. I wanted to give the gift and note to Adira who looked angelic in a peach-coloured coat which matched the colour of her cheeks. Small golden earrings dangled from her earlobes and shone with each of her movements. Her beautiful, glossy hair fell neatly above her breasts and framed her little face. I was beyond mesmerized, just looking at her from afar.

Finally, I managed to wish her happy birthday thirty minutes after she walked in. At that time her friends were still with her, so I could not just hand over the gift to her. 'Thanks, Raunak,' she said with a bright smile and then moved her attention back to her friends. After a while, her friends dispersed from her side, but Sahil and the beefed-up friend of her's ensured that one or the other was with her all the time, giving me no chance to go near her. I envied those two well-dressed men, not only because they were close to Adira but because they could converse freely with attractive females. I, on the other hand, was the least comfortable in that department. *How can I compete with them?* I wondered.

After continuously attempting and failing to go anywhere near, for one hour before as well as after dinner, I decided to quietly slide my gift into her handbag. She was too busy to notice, and I was sure that she would get the opportunity to check her bag only when she was alone in her room. To my surprise, a few minutes after I slid the gift into her purse, she got up to go to the loo and came out beaming with the velvet box in her hand.

Delhi was freezing that night; the temperatures were way below average, yet I felt beads of sweat on my forehead at the sight of her walking back into the room with my gift in her hand. I felt as if something blazing hot had entered my lungs and made me breathless. I was more nervous than I had ever been in my life.

She walked into the sitting area where twenty-odd people were enjoying their drinks and music. Her high-heeled boots went clickety-clack on the marble floor and could be heard despite the loud music in the room.

'What is this?' she asked, looking at no one in particular. She was talking about the gift. No one said a word, and Piyush swiftly lowered the volume of the music system. Adira looked every bit as surprised and intrigued as I had wanted her to be. She sat down on the sofa next to Tamanna and looked at everyone in turn, as if trying to guess just by the faces who had given her the gift.

'Open it and see. There is a note as well,' Rohit cheekily told her, and my face started getting warm.

She carefully pulled out the note from the box and took out her present—a delicate silver charm bracelet. It sparkled beautifully as the numerous lights in the room fell on it from different angles and directions. She traced each charm with her beautiful fingers as if she were kissing them, and then opened the note to read it.

'Read it aloud. We want to hear what it says too,' the beefy boy told her.

She giggled happily and then obliged him. I looked at him in disgust but then quickly turned my eyes to my angel as she read my note. My amateur words came out of her mouth like a beautiful poem:

Dear Adira,
You are the most beautiful girl I have ever seen, and after knowing you the little that I have, I can say that you have the most beautiful heart too.

On this birthday, I hope, wish and pray that you get all that you have ever dreamed, desired and hoped for. May this year be the beginning of the best phase in our life!

P.S. I am not a writer, and words don't come to me quickly. But looking at you, I think someday, I will write a love story.

Love,
A friend

My breath was stuck in my lungs while she read the note, and I softly exhaled on hearing her say, 'Love'.

'Tell me now, who is it from? This is so lovely!' she chirped, looking extremely happy with the surprise.

'You moron. You did not write your name?' Rohit hissed at me in a shallow voice.

'I did not because I will tell her tomorrow. Let her guess and be impatient today. That is my plan!' I whispered back at him grinning.

'It was me,' someone said, and the face-splitting grin disappeared from my face. It was the beefy guy.

'Oh, Nitin!' Adira exclaimed, and all her smiles were suddenly directed towards him. 'Oh, Nitin! You are such a darling! I am blessed to have a friend like you,' she added, and I felt as if all the blood, as well as my life, had been sucked up by the earth in one go.

Lifeless, I looked towards Rohit who annoyingly remarked, 'Well done, Mr Planner. What a jerk you are! You just wasted Rs 2000. Congratulations.'

For the next fifteen minutes, we witnessed Nitin's cheap acting and blushing skills. My head nearly exploded when Adira asked him to put on the bracelet, which he shamelessly did. The girls went ooh and aah over the gesture. Rohit and I took our leave, which no one opposed, and went back to our respective houses in autos.

A little relief came in my direction when fifteen days later I got to know that Nitin had asked Adira to be his girlfriend a few days after the party. She, however, had thought of him as just a good friend and declined his generous offer. The last I knew, the guy had been friend-zoned for life! The bracelet however, still was with her and shone like stars on her slim wrist and, looking at it each time, my heart hummed a love song!

MEETING ROOM NO. 5

BACK TO REALITY

'We are not interested in this job, are we?' Rajbir's question, dipped in sarcasm, hit me hard enough to bring me back into the training room for the rest of the day. My manager had seen me peeking in the direction of the pantry for the fifth time.

'It is not that, sir . . . I . . . I . . .' Why do words fail me each time, especially when I need them the most?

Helplessly, I saw my manager collect his things and stomp out of the room, leaving me alone and clueless about the status of my job. Had I finally managed to get myself kicked out of the position? It appeared that I had.

Within seconds I was running behind Rajbir. There he was! I quickly spotted him and my team, and walked up to him fearing the worst. Thankfully, he was called in for an urgent meeting and had no time to scold me further.

Away from Rajbir's prying eyes, I spent the rest of my day trying to understand the requirements of the client. My main aim that day was to get a new laptop from the administrative team by knocking on several doors, and to get various approvals for a permanent desk assigned to me. I did get a chance to interact with my team members as well who, just like me, were not very fond of talking and making new friends.

I will not lie. After seeing Adira at the pantry, I did get the urge to go and look for her in the training rooms, but I had exhausted my quota of excuses as well as apologies for the day and had to give it a miss. I was unable to spot her anywhere on the floor where I was, for the rest of the day. However, I did find my eyes wandering in the direction of the door as well as the pantry more than a few times while working, in the hope of getting a glimpse of her one more time.

That day I finished work one hour later than the usual time. The training batches left at 8 p.m., and it was 9 p.m. by the time I switched off my new laptop and was packed to head back home. The first thing that I did as soon as I sat in the cab was to dial Rohit's number to find out Adira's whereabouts. Rohit always knew everything about everyone.

Quite unexpectedly, Rohit was too busy to answer my call that evening. I received a text from him five minutes after he disconnected my call: 'Will call back in a while—at a friend's place'. It was unlike him, but I did not stress over it.

Who else could I call to check where Adira is nowadays? I didn't know anyone well enough to be able to check about Adira without them asking me a zillion questions regarding my query. She had changed her mobile number three weeks ago. How did I know that? Her display picture was no longer where it should have been. It was replaced by the image of a pimpled face—an adolescent boy who reminded me of my own schooldays. This happened three weeks ago. *Piyush, yes, he should know as his girlfriend is Adira's best friend—but he is in America.* I dialled his number without giving it a second thought. He picked up the call after the third ring.

'Yo, Brother!' he began in a fake accent.

'It has just been a few months. Where did you pick up this accent from?' I inquired, mainly to tease him.

'What? Shut up!' he sure was not going to let go of the accent any time soon.

'So, how is life?' I had to talk about general things before getting to the point.

'Life is good, but I miss India . . .' There was a hint of sadness which was a first. Piyush managed to stay happy and motivated no matter what the situation was. He was the star of our house, and hearing his voice stricken with sadness and worry was very confusing for me. He was in America; studying and living at the expense of his father. *What else does one want in life?*

'But why?' I asked. 'Isn't America the best place in the world to be? I thought everyone wants to fulfil their big American dream, and you were dying to go to America forever, remember?'

'It is quite amazing, Ronnie. The place is lovely, scenic even. There is great infrastructure in place, the roads are good, people are nice and the weather right now is amazing. But I still feel every now and then that something is missing.'

'What is missing, Bro? Power cuts? Traffic jams?' I teased him.

'No, and for your information—there are traffic jams here as well, terrible ones at certain hours of the day. America is all that I dreamt of, it is what I thought I want, but now I know that it is not what I need. How do I put it—it is not India.' I thought I heard the big boy suppress a sob and decided to lighten his mood a little.

'Do you have a gori (foreigner) girlfriend? Shall I tell Tamanna about her?'

'Shut up!' he was irked by my comment. 'She knows that I will not think of anyone other than her. Moreover, I have something to tell you. But not now.'

'So, what is she up to nowadays?' I asked with genuine curiosity.

He sounded thrilled to talk about Tamanna, and it also achieved my purpose, so I encouraged him to talk more. Piyush informed me that Tamanna had joined a PR company in Gurgaon. And the big news which he wanted to share was that he had decided to visit India in a few months and get married to Tamanna so that he could take her along to America. This was to be announced in a week's time. Then he added that he was late for his school and told me that he had only a few more minutes to talk. *Ask him*, the voice in my head ordered.

'So, do you have any news on Adira?' I asked him, and then held my breath half knowing what was to follow.

'Are you still hung up on her?' I heard him laugh his signature weird laugh for the next few seconds while I continually rolled my eyes at his childish behaviour on the other end. He took a while to settle down and then began with his usual lecture on how I was a fool to be thinking that my one-sided love could get me anything more than pain and embarrassment. Every time this topic came up, he thought it was his duty to remind me about the difference between Adira and me, and how I was not the type of guy a girl like her would want to date. That day, too, our conversation was no different.

How could I tell him that my love for Adira was not dependent or whether it was being nurtured by her love in return? She might or might not love me back as I was not 'her type'. I loved her despite all odds as loving her madly, the way I did, was natural for me. She was like sunshine to me, and I, like a sunflower, was happy looking at her from afar.

I cursed myself through his banter for bringing up Adira's name. I should have waited for Rohit to call me back. If I could, I would have kicked myself in the ass for my impulsiveness. Finally, his time was up; he had to rush to catch his train, so he ended the conversation, telling me that he would let me know if he got to know anything about Adira's present whereabouts, which I knew was a lie. As I put the phone in my pocket, I wondered why there was still no call from Rohit.

I reached home at 10.30 p.m. and went straight into my bedroom. 'Have some food,' my mother called after me, but I bolted the door from inside, telling her that I was not hungry.

'I have had food at work,' I lied to her so that she would not worry all night about me and my empty stomach.

That night, I tossed and turned in my bed, trying to get some rest after a long and tiring day at work, but even sleep was not kind to me. Every time I closed my eyes, Adira's beautiful face popped up in front of me. I recalled the day we had coffee together. No, it was not a date. Well, it was a date, actually; but not ours.

CAFE COFFEE DAY

JANUARY 2016

My one-sided love story had not progressed at all. Still a timid guy, I used to admire Adira from afar and dreamt of confessing my feelings to her one day. When and if that 'one day' would ever come, I was not sure, but I hoped it would come soon enough.

On a cold Sunday afternoon, Tamanna and Piyush planned a coffee date at Cafe Coffee Day, Lajpat Nagar. I got to know, through my personal eavesdropper, Rohit, that Adira was going to accompany Tamanna to the coffee house. I begged Piyush to take me along and lied to him that I had to meet someone at the market and just needed a ride till there. I remember an icy wind was blowing all day, and the sun made an appearance between the clouds once in a while, making the day bearable.

'It is freezing outside, Adira. Sit with us until your friends pick you up,' Tamanna insisted. Adira had plans to go to Saket with a couple of her friends who were coming from Mayur Vihar and were running late.

'Ya, have some warm coffee,' Piyush offered her a seat.

I also took a position at the table, uninvited of course. The lovebirds looked at me with repulsion in their eyes as soon as I sank into the soft sofa. Meanwhile, Adira was busy on her phone.

'Are you not going? You had to meet someone here, right?' Piyush could not resist asking me, and he kicked me hard in the foot under the table.

'Ummm . . . my friends are also stuck in traffic,' I lied with my eyes cast down, pretending to read the menu.

'You can have coffee with us too while you wait,' Tamanna offered politely, and got up with Piyush to order coffee for all four of us.

Adira and I were sitting opposite each other at a table next to the big glass windows with a view of the busy street outside. The winter sun now shone weakly through grey clouds. She stared out of the window, and her eyes flickered as the sunlight glittered on her flawless face. This was the first time I was sitting so close to her. The silver bracelet made delicate sounds every time she tapped her phone with her fingers; the sound was like music to me. She was wearing her usual perfume, and its floral smell calmed me like it always did. Someone came in through the door, and cold wind from outside blew in, tossing her hair all over her face. She moved it aside delicately and looked at me. I was so lost in admiring her that I had not even realized that there were two cups of coffee in front of us already. As our eyes locked, the surroundings disappeared. Suddenly, there was a loud noise as someone's phone buzzed. It was her phone; she got up, leaving me alone at the table, apologizing to Tamanna for not being able to have the coffee as her friends were there to pick her up. I realized then that Tamanna and Piyush were sipping their coffee and cosying up at another table in the corner—it was their date after all.

I did not mind sitting at that table alone, with two cups of coffee and an empty chair. The cups sat untouched for a while. I kept thinking about her; about her almond-shaped eyes that had looked deeply into mine. I picked up one of the cups and raised it to my lips. Till that day I had been quite fond of coffee, but the first sip made me realize how all other drinks had lost their charm for me. I wanted to taste her: her soul, her mind. I wanted to know her more—more than ever.

A WEEK LATER, AT WORK

2017

The week flew by. All I managed to do was sleep, eat, work and call Rohit a few times during the day to check if he had any news on Adira so far. He claimed to know nothing. I hardly had any time to look up from my laptop at work because of my new role. Every night, my shift was longer than usual, and I took a cab back home after everyone else left. Every morning, I reached the metro station with hope in my heart that I would bump into the girl on whose wrist a silver bracelet sparkled brightly. Each morning, as I boarded the metro, my eyes eagerly searched for her, on the platform, in the train and everywhere else, only to be met with disappointment. I had not seen her at work since that day either, and sometimes I wondered if my mind had played a cruel joke on me. *That day when I saw her, was it actually her?* I made one or two futile rounds of the ninth floor, and that was about it. The rational part of me was sure that it was no one else but her, and that I was not mistaken. But my lonely heart was blaming my treacherous mind and urged me to forget it all and move on with my life. *You have too much on your plate already*, my inner voice told me.

Despite having put so much effort into the project, I was not able to submit it on time. It was the last day of the two-day extensions that Rajbir had quite unwillingly granted only because I was new to the team. Finally, at 6 p.m., with a co-worker's help, I managed to complete the task. We cross-checked everything before sending it to Rajbir—*Thank God! I will leave work on time today*—I was relieved.

At 6.30 p.m. sharp, I received an email from my boss, and my plans came crashing down like a house of cards built under a ceiling fan.

Hi Raunak,

I have gone through the email you sent.
Meet me in meeting room number five at 6.45 p.m.

Rajbir

'Shit!' I exclaimed loudly, and apologized immediately for my unruly behaviour at work. I was met with stares from as far as four cubicles away. With apologies pasted all over my face, I sunk as low as I could and reread the email, not that reading it over and over again changed anything.

It did not look like good news. I could almost sense a termination letter coming my way that evening, for I was not being summoned into the wretched meeting room to be praised. That was the moment when I first felt the power of written words; a few written words from one's manager could make one crap in one's pants.

I picked up my laptop and walked towards meeting room number five at the time mentioned in the email. Rajbir was sitting there busily working on his computer. I felt my stomach churn, and terrifying thoughts found their way into my already-messed-up brain. *Are they about to fire me? Oh no! Please no, God. This is my first job! I have not even got my third salary from here*—I offered my prayers to as many gods as I could recall—a practice that I had first begun during my board exams for class ten. I knocked on the glass door very gently with my knuckles, and Rajbir signalled me to come inside and take a seat. I took the empty chair next to the only other person in the room. The other guy gave me a warm smile which I barely managed to return.

'Do you have a passport, Raunak?' Rajbir asked me, and unknowingly pulled the chain on the random train of thoughts which was unnecessarily running through my brain.

'Yes . . . yes, sir.' I managed a response, wondering why I was being asked about my passport.

'I have a replacement here, Mike,' Rajbir said into the phone. That was the moment when I got to know that Rajbir was on a call with a new client again.

Before I could understand anything more, soft sounds at the door broke my concentration. I lifted my head up to see who it was—Adira! As expected, I missed a heartbeat and was sweating behind my ears. She was there. Dressed in a black skirt and crisp white shirt, she looked professional. Her hair was tied back in a ponytail. She stood at the door with another girl who was also dressed in similar attire. The girls looked deeply embarrassed at having disrupted our meeting. Slowly, they walked in, suppressing their smiles, and sank into the two chairs opposite mine—I could see a sheen of sweat on Adira's face. A few strands of hair had escaped her ponytail and fallen on her face. She looked exquisite. Mike was still talking; no one apart from Rajbir was listening to them. The two girls were scribbling notes for each other on a notepad while the guy smirked, reading them from the corner of his eye.

Adira looked in my direction and waved gently. I grinned like a monkey and said, 'Hi.' This was the exact moment when the call ended, and Rajbir cleared his throat to capture the attention of the rest of the people in the room. Unwillingly, I too had to focus my attention in his direction. He stood at the end of the room as he addressed us all. Adira and her friend adjusted their chairs, so we all sat in a row, and she sat next to me at my workplace; giving me jitters.

'So, I guess most of you know why are we here . . .' my boss began.

My eyes wandered towards my neighbour. She had placed her hand on her lap and was examining her fingers. Rajbir paused for a little too long between two statements, and I turned to look at him to know why; only to find him staring back at me arching his left eyebrow—*caught in the act*. Thankfully, he decided to spare me some embarrassment and left me alone.

'As the fourth person in your batch has decided to leave the organization, I have added a member of my existing team to the transitioning batch. Raunak, you need to submit your passport to the admin team tomorrow, and then we will proceed with your movement into this team,' he said, and that was it. Everyone took their leave from the room, and as always, I was left alone with Rajbir who explained to me what had just happened.

A new business had been acquired by the company, and a four-member team had been hired to manage the new clients. Adira was a part of the same team. It was an Australian client, and the new team, along with their managers, was to visit Australia for a month to understand the needs and processes. Due to a personal emergency, one member of the new team had had to leave the company. The client needed only fresh postgraduates to work in the group which was why Rajbir, most unwillingly, had to choose me as a replacement.

I am going to Australia for a month with Adira! It was all too good to be true. As always, the building of grand dream castles began in my head, without much delay. But first, I had to know who was this other overly-friendly guy with whom the two girls giggled non-stop, even after the meeting ended. He looked like a rival to me, and no matter how bad my luck is, my sixth sense never fails me.

Half an hour later, I managed to find out that the guy in Adira's batch was Angad Kapoor—this bit of information was easy to get. He lived in South Extension—I checked his transport roster to get his address and passed it on to Rohit when he finally called me back that same evening. 'Get all the info that you can,' I instructed him. Rohit is a very dependable person when it comes to such detective-like activities. The next day I knew everything I wanted to know about him.

Angad Kapoor
Son of Mr Samarth Kapoor, Advocate, High Court:

Mr Kapoor and his only son were worth so much money that Angad did not need to be working in the company

> that he was working for. Advocate Samarth Kapoor was a very well-known face in Delhi's social circuit as well. Angad's mother was a housewife. Angad had studied in London and had recently come back to India. He wanted to start a consulting firm of his own and decided to work at a similar place to understand what he was getting into.
>
> He knew Adira only at work and had a colourful reputation. Fond of luxury cars, he drove a black BMW X5 to work, and also owned a custom Audi R8.

There was a little more information about his family which Rohit said was juicy but not of any use to us. I knew all that I had to know about him. Not that it made any difference as he was quite far ahead of me in the game. He and Adira took most of their breaks together at work, and he sometimes even dropped her home. 'And by the way, he's a charmer!' Rohit had teased me before hanging up, and I cursed him in my mother tongue, in whispers, so that my mother didn't hear.

INDIRA GANDHI INTERNATIONAL AIRPORT, NEW DELHI TWO WEEKS LATER (2017)

The rest of the team was already in Australia. I was the last person to be picked for the team, and the paperwork had taken forever, so they had to leave without me three days ago. My ticket and visa had arrived the evening before, and I was at the airport waiting to board my flight. I arrived there a little early and had to kill time by roaming around. Later, after obtaining my boarding pass, I was free from my luggage and walked into a bookstore. I found many romance books beautifully lined up on the shelves but decided to pick up a book from the humour section instead. It was a satire on Godmen in India and had a quirky cover. It was going to be a long flight, and the baba on the cover looked like a worthy companion.

Finally, at 9 a.m., I boarded my Jet Airways flight. It was till Singapore, where I was going to board a second plane which would take me to Tullamarine Airport, Melbourne.

With all the last-minute formalities and late-night packing, I had not managed to get enough sleep the previous night. My mother had woken me up an hour before the time that I asked her to as she feared I might miss my first international flight. This had further shortened my already short nap. The doors closed, I put my mobile phone in flight mode and fastened my seat belt, hoping to catch up on some sleep before I began reading the book. The announcements started, and the flight attendants went through their drill. It was my first ever international flight—but instead of being happy and taking tens and hundreds of selfies like most of the other passengers, I was bracing myself for the take-off. I knew that kids howled when taking off due to a change in the air pressure. Next to me was a family with a small child who looked angelic and continuously gave me a toothless smile. The plane finally began to ascend.

Fortunately, the child's mother was well prepared. She stuffed the child's mouth with a milk bottle, and he did not cry during take-off, but many other babies did. We flew away from Delhi, and sleep flew away from my eyes. I took out my book and began to read as sleeping was out of the question after all the hustle and bustle. The gang of babies was at work non-stop until we landed.

THE TINY TRANSIT

CHANGI AIRPORT

I had very little time to explore Changi airport but I can tell you that it is anything but boring. It is proof that airports don't necessarily have to just be a complex of runways and buildings like most airports in the world are.

I wandered aimlessly for some half an hour while deciding on what to eat and got a sneak peek of its butterfly habitat and pool. After I grabbed a quick warm meal at one of the fast food restaurants, I headed back to my terminal. The place was buzzing with people from around the globe who were occupied in amusements like movie theatres, snooze lounges, spas and everything else that one can imagine. I got so engrossed in looking around that I lost my way back to my terminal and had to seek help from a staff member in a pink and purple blazer. She navigated through her iPad and gave me directions. Thankfully, I was where I was supposed to be just in time to catch the flight.

The first leg of my journey was over, and I was only six and a half hours away from Adira. I finished reading my book in the waiting area. It was nearly time for the next flight. I prayed to God for no more babies to be close to where I was seated as I was in dire need of some sleep.

Thankfully, I was seated in the fourth row. The seats next to me were all empty. The flight was under-booked. Despite the lack of leg room, I managed to make myself comfortable by propping up my legs. I unpacked the blanket, adjusted the small pillows under my back and wandered into the world of my dreams.

TULLAMARINE AIRPORT, MELBOURNE

I collected my luggage from the belt—two black suitcases—and I already had a backpack. Once I managed to get it all, I headed out. As per the last information shared with me by the travel team in India, a chauffeur from the company was to pick me up and drop me at the apartment-hotel where everyone else was staying.

For about the tenth time I counted my bags standing alongside the taxi belt—one, two, three. Honestly, had I lost anything during transit or while waiting for the chauffeur, it would have made a great story to tell to the future generations but nothing of that sort happened. By the time my plane landed, my stomach was doing flips and as I arrived at the exit gate nervousness took over me. For the first time in my life I was going to be exposed to a little taste of what the real world is like, away from friends and family; I was anxious to finally grow up.

As I stood waiting for a taxi outside of the airport, it was immediately apparent to me that Melbourne was something else, it was not like any place that I had been before. At the airport, it seemed like everyone there was in a hurry to get to another place. After around ten minutes, I was greeted by an Indian guy who was impeccably dressed in a grey suit. He held my name-card which had a wrong spelling of my name on it. He greeted me in limited yet accented English and shook my hand. I asked him his name, 'Gurjeet Singh, sir,' he said, and bent down to pick up my bags.

'Are you really a chauffeur?' I asked him as we hit the road.

'Yes, sir' he replied with pride, and then went on to explain. 'There is nothing wrong with any job, sir. I drive cabs as it pays well. Better than my previous job. Moreover, I like the feeling of being my own boss,' he told me without taking his eyes off the road.

'Yes, I agree,' I said, a little embarrassed by my question. *No job is small; no role is insignificant. Every position has its importance in the world. Your post doesn't define you; you define yourself.* My grandfather's words came back to me. He had started work as a mason and eventually left property worth crores for his family—all because of his hard work and determination. What happened to the property worth crores? Well, *that* is a different story.

I admired the natural beauty on both sides of the road as we drove. Long stretches of green land, fewer cars than one is used to seeing in India and a bright-blue sky. It was 7 a.m., and the sun was out. The early morning sun had bathed everything golden. I rolled down the window on my side and let the pleasantly cool breeze caress my face. It was quite similar to the monsoon winds. Thinking about the monsoon winds, my tired but idle mind drifted back in time.

NEW DELHI, INDIA

AUGUST 2016

Tamanna had just moved out of my nani's house. Her parents had bought her an apartment in Greater Noida. She now lived there with one of her cousins and her younger brother, Sumit. Tamanna was offering Adira a space in her new home at a much lower price than she was paying Nani—this news travelled from Tamanna to Piyush to Rohit and finally to me.

'What did Adira say? Is she moving out?' I asked Rohit desperately.

'What is it to you? It is not as if she stays here, you are going to ask her out, is it?' He did not miss any opportunity to rub salt in my open wounds. After the disaster on Adira's birthday, I had decided to move on with things at a pace I was comfortable with. And I knew that I was not comfortable talking to her, let alone asking her out.

'Tamanna asked Adira to only pay her share of the household expenses and live with her, but Adira declined her offer as her father is not comfortable with her sharing a house with a boy, even if it is her best friend's cousin,' Rohit told me after a few moments of silence.

I was happy to hear that because it meant Adira was not moving out, but I did not show it in front of Rohit. I pretended to remain grumpy until he said sorry for his harsh words earlier, although I knew he was not.

We walked idly in front of Nani's house, eating bhutta (corn) and chatting. I hoped to get a glimpse of Adira. I had not seen her for two weeks. She had gone to Chandigarh to visit her family for a week, and the day she came back, my parents decided it was time to go on a long-awaited trip to Vaishno Devi. We went by train to Punjab and halted at a relative's place while going to Jammu as well as on the way back. I prayed to Goddess Durga to give me courage and enough charm to woo the girl of my dreams, half hoping that such requests were also considered matters of urgency and the wish would be granted to me swiftly.

That evening did not turn out to be fruitful as Adira locked herself in her room. Nani's maid knocked on Adira's door, asking her to come out for lunch as well as dinner, but she asked her to bring some warm water and tea instead. I saw the maid walk out of Adira's room and head towards the kitchen to prepare tea for her. That was when I began my interrogation.

'What happened to the madam upstairs?' I asked Nani's maid, trying to sound as casual as possible.

'I do not know. She looks unwell—a cold maybe,' she informed me casually, and continued cooking in the kitchen.

It was 9 p.m. My mother had called me a few times already, asking me to come home for dinner. She had made chicken that evening, which was my favourite. 'I will be back soon,' I told her, and hung up. I dashed to the nearby medical store and came back with a few paracetamol tablets, cold & flu tablets and cough drops.

Very gently, I knocked on the door of Adira's room. Nani did not like any boy, even her grandsons, going anywhere near her PG's apartment, and I was playing with fire. Getting caught would mean being reported to my mother, which was also dangerous. But I had to check on her and give her those medicines.

After a few knocks, she answered and told me that the door was open. I lightly pushed the door with my hands. The lights in the room had been dimmed, and I could barely see her. 'Who is it?' she asked. Her nose seemed stuffed, and her voice sounded funny but cute. I lifted my left foot to walk in and then placed it back on the ground; I did not want a scandal—neither for her nor for myself.

'I have got some medicines for your cold, and there is one if you also have some fever,' I said, standing at the door.

'Oh, thanks. Rohit, is it?' she asked me. I am sure she was not able to recognize me or my voice in the dark. And I did not bother to clarify; it did not matter who she thought I was. All that mattered was that she got the medicines as she was not well.

'Nani doesn't like a guy in her PG's room, so I am handing over the medicines to the maid. She will bring them to you with some ginger tea,' I told her, and turned around.

'Thanks!' I heard her murmur in a sleepy voice as I headed down the stairs.

The next day, I went in the morning to check how she was feeling and whether she took the medicines I had bought for her the previous night. To my surprise, dressed in a matching pink pyjama set, she stood outside sipping tea with Rohit. She looked a little paler than usual, but her voice sounded much better than the night before. They were both chatting with ease.

'Hello, Adira, how are you today?' I mustered enough courage and blurted out the line I had practised the entire night.

'I am good now, thanks!' she answered me with a smile.

'Okay, I will see you guys later,' she said to Rohit in particular and waved at me. She gently touched Rohit's shoulder and gave him an extra bright smile before leaving.

'So, what was that all about?' I asked the stupidly grinning monkey who happened to be my cousin.

'She was telling me how she loves the rains and monsoon winds, and that she was out in the rain with her college friends which is the reason why she caught a cold,' he said, looking slyly at me.

'Okay.' I enjoyed hearing about Adira any time of the day, but the sight of her hand brushing his shoulder made me uncomfortable.

'—And she was thanking me,' he added.

'Why was she thanking you?'

'For the medicines,' he replied shamelessly.

'What! You bastard! I was the one who got the medicines for her!'

'I know, but she thinks it was me.'

'Why didn't you tell her that it wasn't?' I inquired irritably.

'To teach you a lesson that you need to tell her things yourself,' he said, and ran as fast as he could. I ran in the same direction to beat the shit out of him.

He was the least fit person I knew, and as expected, he was panting like a dog by the time he reached the end of the lane. I caught hold of him by his collar.

'Achoooo!' he sneezed loudly. It looked like Adira's flu had passed on to him.

'God has his ways, my friend. Enjoy the flu,' I told him, and walked back home. He deserved the cold he had caught—a little punishment for hiding the truth. Since that day, I believe in karma.

'Achoooo . . .' The chauffeur's sneeze brought me back to Melbourne.

MELBOURNE CBD

Welcome to the city, sir,' Gurjeet said, looking at me in the rear-view mirror and smiling.

I looked around. Unlike the places we crossed to reach our destination, the city was full of people and buildings. There were trams and buses everywhere. It was quite early in the morning, yet I could see a lot of people on the roads.

'So, this is CBD, is it?' I inquired.

'Yes, sir, and you are going to love it,' Gurjeet said with pride.

I was too tired to love the place then, but I must tell you that I did fall in love with it eventually. It is a comforting place—as reassuring as a warm cup of coffee on an icy-cold evening. It had a special place in my heart, and I would cherish every moment spent there for the rest of my life.

I was free that day and had to join the rest of the team at work the next day. We parked outside the hotel, and Gurjeet helped me carry my luggage. I read the name of the hotel just before entering it—Punthill Apartment Hotel, Flinders Street. I was given a card for my apartment, and a valet took my luggage upstairs to the fifth floor. Before I left, I was told that two people were to stay in one serviced apartment together.

The red-haired valet and I reached the fifth floor. I placed my white key card on the reader, and the door of room number 350 opened. We walked into a spacious living room. A brown three-seater leather couch and a beautiful wooden centre table made the room look comfortable and cosy. In front of the sofa were two big glass windows with an incredible view of the calm Yarra river. There was a large TV and a dining table as well as a few abstract paintings.

It looked pleasant and quiet. As we moved towards the bedroom, I felt a wave of tiredness wash over me. Signalling the valet to leave the bags in the corner, I sat heavily on the white linen bedcover. As soon as he left the room, I flopped back on the cosy bed. I cannot recall anything after that because the last thing I know is that I had crashed with my face at an awkward angle on the pillow and my legs dangling under the bed.

I woke up with a jolt after a bad dream. I saw myself hanging from a parachute as there was a problem with the plane I was in. The flight attendants asked us all to fold our legs, but as soon as I did so, my seat flew into the sky, and I was dropping freely. When I woke up, I was still dressed in the same clothes which I had put on the previous morning, and I was sweating profusely after the nightmare. I was in dire need of a shower. I got up from the bed and wiped the drool from the corner of my mouth.

Behind the headboard was a wall, and on it was a painting of a flower which at first glance looked like a heart to me. This is the thing with the human brain—it shows you what you want to see, everywhere. Excited about the next many days to come, all I could see was hearts.

I walked up to the window and thought about how life had planned everything for me: my meeting with Adira, her working at my office, my coming to Melbourne with her. Ideally, I should have come to Australia with a plan, but I had not. *Why?* Because I had recently learnt that you do not always need a plan. Sometimes all you need is a little trust. Trust what life offers you, take a deep breath and let go of all your inhibitions. Once you do that, life presents to you all the miracles it is capable of.

This was precisely what I was going to do: relax and let life take control of itself.

By 6 p.m., I had taken the much-needed shower, changed into a fresh set of clothes and made a call to my mother who was only concerned about the food which I had or hadn't eaten. 'I have had some sandwiches, Ma . . .' I assured her, and started describing the view from my window. My mother, however, was stuck at the word 'sandwiches'. For the next five minutes, she told me how careless my eating habits were. She only dropped the topic when I promised that I would eat something more substantial after the call. After about half an hour, there was a knock at the door. By then, I was sitting in front of the TV stuffing my mouth with a red velvet cake. The door opened, and I saw my roommate standing there—it was Rajbir.

'Sir . . .' I said, which sounded more like 'fur' with all the food stuffed in my mouth. Just then some crumbs from the cake also decided to fall from my mouth and land on the cream carpet. I stood there embarrassed.

'I see you have made yourself comfortable already, haven't you?' his tone was sarcastic. I did not make any attempt to say anything more. Thankfully, leaving me in the company of food, Rajbir walked into his bedroom without saying anything more.

Later that evening, Rajbir and I sat at the dining table facing each other. He looked relaxed in his PJs. I fiddled with a piece of decoration, a white and blue miniature sand clock, waiting for him to begin a conversation.

'So, how was your flight?' he finally asked me, taking his eyes off his phone.

'It was good, thanks,' I replied. There was nothing more to add.

His phone rang. The team had planned to go out and eat south Indian food for dinner that evening. We got up to get dressed.

'Chalo, let's go,' Rajbir said as soon as we were ready. We locked the door behind us. Adira and her friend, whose name was Sakshi, came out of their room. They were staying next door to us.

I eyed Adira. She was dressed in a baby-blue dress, her hair was tied in a bun, and she looked beautifully carefree and relaxed. Sakshi was chatting animatedly next to her. I do not recall much of what she said to me when we met as I had eyes only for Adira.

Then Adira extended her hand to greet me. 'How was the flight?' she asked me casually as I placed my hand in hers. Her soft palms touched mine, and for the first time it felt like something had happened that went beyond words. I froze at the contact. I bet she noticed it because I saw her blush. *Why would she blush at a touch from you? Look at her and look at you. She is perfect while you are anything but perfect for her*—I came back to my senses exactly when I felt Rajbir's eyes on me. I was still holding Adira's hand. I quickly withdrew it, and we all walked out. That touch had, however, made me even more conscious of Adira. As I walked with her next to me, I could feel her.

At the restaurant, I was quiet during most of the dinner, mainly because I was very conscious of Rajbir's attentiveness towards my actions. Somehow, he caught me every time I looked at Adira and raised his eyebrows. His reaction made me very nervous. I dropped everything which came into contact with my hands. Adira was her usual chirpy self. She laughed at every joke Angad made. Her closeness with Angad added to my discomfort, and I was unable to eat properly.

'You have hardly eaten,' Sakshi commented on my barely touched plate, and I blamed my lack of appetite on jet lag.

Finally, Rajbir paid the bill. Three meals every day were to be paid by the company for every employee, and that dinner went on to the same account.

All of us headed back to the hotel, and we quickly dispersed into our rooms as it was quite late by then.

Rajbir worked on his laptop till late in the night, and I do not remember when I fell asleep looking at the book which I had started reading on the plane. Its cover had a picture of a very funny-looking Godman, and I drifted into my past, recalling my tryst with a Godman in India.

MY ALMOST MEETING WITH A GODMAN
NEW DELHI, INDIA
OCTOBER 2016

Nothing in my life was going as per my plans. I wondered if making plans made any sense. My studies had gone haywire, and Adira had found a boyfriend. It was a week ago when Rohit broke the news to me that Adira was dating a man who'd been dropping her at Nani's house from her college quite frequently in his white Swift Dzire. The worst thing was that this courting was arranged by her parents—yes, she was meeting a man whom her parents thought to be good enough for her to get married to. Rumour had it that the beautiful pair was to get married as soon as she finished her studies, provided all went well between them. I was broken to say the least. I knew that I had taken forever to tell her how I felt about her, but I had my reasons. I was very low on confidence, and was scared that she would never give me a chance to even confess my feelings for her the way I wanted to. So I tried hard to forget her. Little did I know that my feelings for her were seeds which when buried deep in my heart, would grow into love.

I tried to drink and smoke to forget her, but it didn't bring any relief as her face remained in front of my eyes all the time, and the fact that she was going to be someone's wife in a few months brought tears to my eyes. I bunked college on the days when I had to attend classes as per the pact with my friends. Soon those college friends too left my side.

I thought of various ways to smother my love for her, but the truth is that true love never dies. It sleeps silently in aching hearts and wakes up on lonely nights. These nights were what I dreaded the most. I began sharing my pain and heartbreak with Rohit, but very soon he was on the brink of getting too frustrated with me to care.

'Why did she do this to me, yaar?' I asked him, again and again, one drunk night on the roof of his house.

'She did nothing! The fact is that you did nothing when you could have,' his words were harsh but true, and I agreed with him somewhere deep inside. I knew that I had not given myself a chance when there was time.

'Can I do something now? Do you think if I tell her how I feel about her, would she be interested? Do you think I stand a chance at all?'

'Are you crazy? Have you seen the guy her parents have chosen for her?' *Why are all his words making sense tonight?* The guy was rich, good-looking and from what I saw from afar, he cared for her too.

'What if I tell this guy that Adira and I are having an affair and that he should get out of the way? No one wants to get married to someone else's girlfriend!' I blurted out the stupid plan that had been brewing in my head for the past week.

'Listen to yourself! You have stooped so bloody low! How can you think of lying? Moreover, I do not think he will believe you. This is not a movie. Only a miracle can work things out for you now. And as we all know, there is no such thing in the world as a miracle, so it is better that you move on now. . . .' he went on, but I lost him there.

'Miracle, miracle . . .' I repeated a few times before passing out.

The next day when I woke up, the word miracle was still stuck in my head. I was sleeping on a folding bed on the rooftop. Rohit was snoring next to me on the floor. His father and mother were downstairs. It was quite early in the morning, so instead of waking up my super-intelligent cousin, I formulated a plan. A lot of Godmen claim to help lovers through some small *upaaye* (remedy). Lovers like me, the ones who love with all their heart, one-sidedly—my kind of lovers—approach Godmen to get the love of their lives to love them back, and then they live happily ever after! Magic was the only thing I could count on in my circumstances. I decided to find one such baba on the Internet and see if he could help me. Like a cat in super-stealth mode, I left Rohit's house quietly and went home to organize the next step.

In the afternoon, after having lunch with my parents, I stepped out of the house with a telephone number scribbled on a small piece of crumpled paper and called the baba. His secretary picked up the call and asked me to let her know about the problem. I told her my sad story, remembering to change the names of all the major characters. 'Come and meet us at our office,' she said after listening to my saga of love, as I prefer to call it. 'And get at least thirty strands of the girl's hair,' she told me before hanging up. *It is not a big deal; it is just hair,* I told myself. My scared heart was suddenly not so sure of what I was getting myself and Adira into.

Rohit had called me a few times since I'd sneaked out of his home without waking him up; he wanted to check on me and see if I was okay. I called him back and assured him that all was fine. After having a cup of tea, I decided to go to Nani's home to complete the mission. I tiptoed up the stairs and reached Adira's room. A dustbin was kept outside the room, and I hoped to find my treasure in it—thirty or more strands of her hair. *The door is closed, great! That makes my work easy.* I lifted the lid and scanned the contents of the bin with a lot of concentration leaving aside the disgust.

Suddenly, I heard a voice coming from Adira's room; she was not alone. Tamanna was with her, and she sounded outraged, 'What a swine! How could he?' I froze as soon as I heard her. *Hurry up*, my mind said, or you will get caught peeping in the dustbin like a starving cat.

'Do not talk about him please, Tamanna. I tried to make it work, but he said that I was not worth his time and that he is calling it off!' Adira was weeping. Her voice was low, the saddest I had ever heard her. I left the task at hand and ran down the stairs; her words echoed in my head, and my heart thumped fast. I was so close to being caught with my hand in the dustbin of the girl I claimed to love when she was going through a crisis. *I am such an ass!* I thought, *only thinking about myself.* I looked at my reflection in the mirror with loathing for what I had become. I was planning to practise magic on the girl I claimed to be in love with. I never thought about her: her feelings, her emotions. I stayed away from Adira, and for the next few days I could not even meet my own eyes in the mirror. I was thankful that I had not disclosed this dirty little secret to anyone, and it will go with me to the grave.

The sound of my phone vibrating brought me back to the present—to my apartment in Melbourne. I looked at Rajbir's bed. It was neatly made up, and he was nowhere to be seen. I wondered if he had already left for work. I had to reach work at 8 a.m., and the office was only a ten-minute walk from the hotel. I picked up my shaving kit and walked into the washroom. On the mirror was a note for me:

> It can be just one day or day one . . . It is for you to decide. Meet me in the coffee shop if you are ready for day one—Rajbir

I read and reread the note to make sense of it.

CONFESSIONS OF A BROKEN HEART

Rajbir sat alone in the corner of the fancy coffee shop on the ground floor of the building. He had chosen a table overlooking the street. He was staring very intently at something outside and did not notice my arrival. 'Good morning, sir,' I said to bring him back from wherever he had mentally escaped to.

'Good morning,' he said, turning his face towards me. I noticed an empty coffee cup on the table and wondered how early he must have woken up to have been dressed and out here. He had even had a cup of coffee before 7.15 a.m., while I had skipped my shower to be on time to meet him. *I had already taken a shower yesterday evening*—a perfect excuse was handy. I had quickly slipped into a formal brown shirt and beige trousers, and rushed downstairs to find out if the note meant what I thought it did, and if so, I was ready to make it day one of my life—provided we were talking about the same thing.

I took a seat opposite Rajbir and placed his note on the table. 'I am a very private person, but I think you need to hear this story as it would help you in doing the right thing,' he said. I looked at him blankly, and he went on to tell me a sweet love story. 'So, there was this boy—happy and jovial. He was adored by his friends, boys as well as girls. He had a friend whom he had known as long as he'd known himself. She was his neighbour and classmate. They spent their evenings together playing and fighting as kids and discussing studies, exams and tuition classes as teenagers. The boy knew that he loved this girl very much,' he said after a pause, and removed an invisible piece of thread from his trousers, distracting me. Then he cleared his throat and continued, 'He believed that the girl also loved him, as much as he loved her if not more. But they never spoke about it. He never thought that there was any need to talk about what was as obvious as the rising and setting of the sun. They finished school and joined different colleges. Naturally, they met new people—the guy, because of his smooth talking and confidence, befriended girls easily. He knew how to woo them, and soon he had more than a few girlfriends. In short, he was an arsehole.' He laughed a sad laugh and looked away.

'And then?' I prompted him when he paused for too long.

'Then one day, this girl saw the boy with one of his many girlfriends. He had never told her how much he loved her. She assumed that he didn't and that she was in a one-sided love affair. She stopped talking to the boy. All his charm and tactics failed in front of the girl he loved. At her parents' persistence, she agreed to get married to an NRI who lived in the UK and went away from his life forever, all within three months.'

'What happened to the boy, sir?' I couldn't help but ask about the fate of the boy who could not confess his feelings in time.

'He died a death every night thinking about her, recalling the times she'd let him hold her hands; the times they'd gazed together at the stars and wished one would fall so that they could wish for togetherness for eternity—without telling each other. The boy still stalks her Facebook account to get a glimpse of her. He wanted to get the moon for her once, and now he looks at the moon and tries to see her face in it.'

'How are you so sure that the girl loved the boy if she agreed to get married to someone else?' I had to ask this, as somewhere in my heart I knew that Rajbir was narrating his own tale of love.

'I know because she told me she did. Before she left, she wrote a note:

> When I am gone, don't look for me. A part of me will always be with you . . .

'After receiving the note, I ran straight to her house. She was the bride to be and as expected was surrounded by her relatives and friends. We had been friends for so long that no one found it weird that I wanted to talk to her, alone. She didn't want to talk at first while I tried to make her say something. When there was a knock at the door to tell her that it was time to visit the jeweller, she broke down. Crying on my shoulders, she told me how much she loved me and how she thought I did not. I tried to convince her that I loved her. But there was not enough time, the wedding was in a week's time. Also, she told me that I was too late in confessing my feelings for her, and things were no longer as they once had been—she had decided to find love in the eyes and heart of the person her parents thought was fit to be her partner for life. "It is not that simple any more," she told me, and I can't blame her. It was all my fault that I'd taken her love for granted.'

I was shocked listening to the confession of my manager, and I saw the handsome, intelligent Rajbir break down in front of me.

Suddenly, I felt as if someone had hit me hard. *Was I taking too long? Was I so worried about rejection that I was not even giving it a try? What if Adira also gets married?* I instantly decided that I needed to give myself a chance. I did not know if she would say yes or no, but until I asked her, I would never find out. But I knew it would take me some time.

'Sir, I do not think that you and I have anything in common,' I told him sadly. I am shy and an introvert, while Rajbir was nothing like me.

'I know,' he said, and he told me something that I can never forget. His words were inspiring, and I have been practising what he said ever since, not just with Adira but with everything else in my life as well. Later, I noted down the words as I would remember them:

> 'The answer is "no" until you ask. When you ask, you give "yes" a chance. There is a 50 per cent probability that the odds will be in your favour. Always give the other person a chance to choose between a "yes" and a "no" for you, for your love; instead of choosing a "no" yourself. I am sure you would have heard that saying that an "oops" is way better than a "what if". I am a "what if"— what if I had asked her out? What if I had told her about my feelings? Do not be me. Do not be a "what if".' His words made sense, and I finally knew what I

had to do. 'The mind governs it all. If your mind tells you that you can do it, trust me, nothing can stop you.' His final advice gave me a lot to think about. That day, during my break I found myself making mental notes of what I loved the most about Adira—the list was endless. That is where I needed to start.

The rest of my day went by in catching up with the batch. Samantha, a tall, blonde trainer, took me through the modules I had missed.

'We are planning to go to a Melbourne Central for some shopping,' the girls announced in a chorus on our way back from the office. Of course, Angad was accompanying the girls! And naturally, I was not thrilled about it. It probably showed because Rajbir asked me, 'All okay, tiger?' placing a hand on my shoulder. Despite our conversation in the morning, I could not bring myself to discuss my personal life with him. He was my manager, after all.

'Yeah . . .' I replied, sulking.

'She does seem to be very fond of Angad,' Rajbir said to me, out of the blue over dinner. 'Jealousy will take you nowhere. She has a life, and will always have friends. Some of them will be men, while some will be women. If you want her to love you back and respect you, then the first thing you need to do is to chuck the word insecurity out of your dictionary. I understand that girls like their guys to be involved, and a little insecurity is cute but just in the beginning. As the relationship grows, it is this insecurity which causes the most harm. As a man, have confidence in yourself, and trust her enough to let her have friends.'

'But we are not in a relationship yet,' I corrected him.

'Exactly! You are not even in a relationship with her, and you have a problem with her friends. Just imagine how quickly this will drive the girl away.' He was right, but old habits die hard. I did resolve to work on it though.

That night too Rajbir worked on his laptop, while I thought of ways to get to know Adira more, little by little. I still believed that the key to successfully beginning a conversation with a girl was with a compliment.

WHEN I WAS LEARNING TO LOVE

The next day, I went to work with a compliment ready in my mind. *I shall say it to her the moment I see her*, I decided. But nothing goes as per my plan, does it? I sat next to her through all the training, and the group had lunch together, so I had more than a few chances to tell her, and yet I couldn't. Why? Because every time I looked into her eyes, they made me forget the world.

My dad had once told me to fake confidence. 'How do I do that?' I remember asking him innocently.

'Close your eyes and visit your happy place,' he'd responded.

'Okay, here we go,' I said aloud to myself, sitting alone in the room that night after dinner, and I closed my eyes to visit my happy place. My happy place was the time when I had accidentally managed to accompany Adira and her friends to Goa, this was after her break-up. One evening while all of us were merrily partying in a shack, Adira walked out alone to take a stroll along the beach.

I too left my seat and walked to the stairs, but I did not follow her. I saw her walking along the beach, with her slippers in her hand. The water touched her beautiful feet as if the sea were kissing them. Slowly, as the minutes passed by, the orange sun melted into the deep-blue ocean, painting the sky in different shades of red—the colour of love. Soon, the ocean and the sun became one, and the place became darker, giving them the privacy they needed. Distant rays fell on Adira's face, making her look even more beautiful. All I could hear was the crash of waves rising and falling like a song; all my eyes could see was Adira, at a distance. She closed her eyes to savour the beauty of love, and I closed mine to freeze the moment forever, and this has been my happy place ever since.

The next morning, coincidentally, I bumped into Adira at the coffee shop at the apartment building. She was dressed in a formal dark-blue dress and blazer. I instantly noted that she was looking different that day. Her hair was tied in a ponytail, and she reminded me of the early morning sun—bright, warm and enigmatic. We sat at the same table, and once our order had arrived I grabbed her attention. There she sat, opposite me, looking pretty as a picture. I felt my heart thump so hard that it would have burst out of my chest, had it been possible. 'Blue suits you,' I told her in a low voice, and in my heart, I knew this was the beginning of a new relationship for us. How? You may ask. It was the way she replied that told me. Adira tilted her head slightly and thanked me with the brightest smile, and then started fidgeting with her coffee.

That day we took our lunch break together at work, thanks to Rajbir, and chatted our half an hour away. We mainly spoke about Piyush and Tamanna, but it is still one of the most memorable times in Melbourne for me.

Days passed, and conversations with her became more exciting and personal. A week later, Adira planned an outing for all of us. 'Let's go to St Kilda Beach,' she suggested, and everyone agreed. However, I was in no mood to go out in such a big group, and when I voted out, she walked up to me at work and jolted my world.

'Raunak, are we not friends?' she asked me. Friends? *No, I dream about you way too often for us to be just friends,* I wanted to scream. I did not want her to friend-zone me. I had been lingering somewhere in that zone for so many years! *How do I tell her to not see me as a friend?* I wondered as she stood over my desk.

'What happened?' I asked her, instead of responding to her question and starting a war of words. I kept my eyes constantly glued to my computer screen. I could still feel her glaring eyes shooting daggers at me.

'Why are you not coming with us to the beach?'

To avoid being just a friend—I want more, I wish I could have said that. 'I need to visit a temple instead,' I lied, knowing very well that she was a religious girl and the excuse would spare me any further questioning.

To my surprise, she replied, 'I too have wanted to go to a temple ever since I came here. Why didn't you ask me? I thought you knew that I usually visit a temple every weekend!'

I had to take my eyes away from the flat screen and look at her then; her voice had a sudden sadness in it. I had never heard her sound so disappointed. *Is she disappointed in me for not asking her out? Or for forgetting that she visits a temple? Does she expect me to remember such things about her?* I did remember that she visits a temple every weekend, but I did not take the fact into account while making up an excuse. Honestly, I had no plans. I did not know where to find a temple in Melbourne, or even if there were any.

'I am sorry . . .' that was all I could mutter after getting drenched in guilt from her words. 'Would you like to come along?' I asked her, trying my luck at some damage control.

'Yes, of course, you idiot!' she replied in excitement, and pressed my hand. All my life, I have despised the word—idiot—but coming from her mouth, it sounded like the sweetest sound in the world. Butterflies danced in my stomach, and the world around me spun at a speed unknown to mankind.

'What about St Kilda?' I asked her, forcing the stuck breath out of my lungs. By then Adira had already walked four cubicles away.

'I hate beaches,' she said, and turned around, dazzling me with her smile. And like that, my friend, a day at work was successfully wasted. I could think of nothing else. I got no work done and hardly ate. My mind kept replaying her words, and my senses fooled me by revisiting the sensation of her hand on mine.

That night I didn't sleep a wink. No, my brain was not still acting up. I was up and awake because I could not find a mandir anywhere in Melbourne where I could take her. My Indian colleagues mostly stayed forty to fifty minutes away from the city and hardly visited temples. Google searches do not help you when you need them to. Finally, at 3 a.m., I found what I was looking for. I dozed off next to my laptop on the sofa and was woken up by my manager the next day with a jolt.

It was 8.30 a.m., and I had promised Adira to meet her at 9 a.m. in the cafe. Late as always, I sprang up from my bed and quickly took a shower. I put on my favourite pair of jeans—they were my favourites because they were the only pair I owned. I chose a red T-shirt to slip over them and was ready. I didn't have a lot of time to check or improve my appearance as I already had three missed calls and a couple of messages from my lady. Yes, we had exchanged numbers only last night, and one more reason why I was up till 3 a.m. was that I was constantly checking her display picture and status on WhatsApp—I was as love-struck as one could be! I browsed the messages quickly. One said that she was furious as I was not picking up her calls, and the second was to tell me that she was waiting for me in the coffee shop. It was delivered two minutes ago, and I was relieved. I wasn't that late after all.

WHEN I FELL IN LOVE WITH HER—ALL OVER AGAIN

Missing a few stairs and escaping a couple of falls, I managed to reach the coffee shop unhurt. The place was deserted at 9 a.m., which was quite a contrast from what I was used to seeing. It was usually full of people all hours of the day. It was a Saturday morning, and most people either begin their day late or super early on weekends in Melbourne. Adira sat at the corner table. It had an unhindered view of the street outside, which was also quiet as compared to the other days. She felt my presence in the coffee shop as I walked towards her, and turned her face towards me. I froze midway and could not take my eyes off her. She was dressed in a bright-yellow salwar suit with her beautiful, long hair spread loosely over her back. She looked more beautiful than I had ever seen her before. Adira gave me a warm smile. I observed that her almond-shaped eyes were beautifully lined with dark streaks of kajal. She also wore a sparkly golden bindi on her forehead. It was not the first time I had seen her dressed in traditional Indian wear, but the way she sat there was pretty as a picture; she looked like an artist's muse—captivating and alluring.

There is a certain charm in the way she looks at me, or at anyone for that matter, and I would never be able to explain it to anyone. No words can do justice to the feelings which rose in my heart when she looked directly at me, inviting me into her beautiful world.

I saw a small frown appear on her forehead, maybe because I had been staring at her for too long or probably because my mouth was open in surprise. 'Is something the matter?' she asked me as politely as she could, embarrassing me.

'No . . . no.' I bowed my head to hide my embarrassment, and waited for her to get up. I had called for an Uber which was waiting for us outside, to take us to the Sai Temple.

'You look so . . . beautiful!' I finally managed to tell her once we were inside the cab. There was an awkward silence hanging in the air before and after the words were spoken. But I was happy that I had told her what I felt, for better or for worse.

She took it genuinely, and smiled and said, 'Thank you!'

The temple was half an hour's journey from our apartment. In fact, I realized that everything was half an hour to forty-five minutes distance from where we were—malls, parks, the zoo, a temple—I mean everything!

I aimed to utilize our time together in the cab by trying to know more about her, but as always my plans that day too did not work. Even before I could adjust myself next to Adira inside the cab, Adira established that the cab driver was an Indian and was in fact from her own city—Chandigarh. The rest of our trip was very pleasant for the two of them as they spoke at length about each other while I looked for opportunities to butt into the conversation every once in a while. Both of them politely ignored me and my failed attempts as they discussed Chandigarh and everything about it. Finally, we reached there in what felt like ages to me. We got down, and she bid goodbye to her city buddy. Adira respectfully covered her head with a dupatta that she was carrying in her purse, and we walked into a building which looked like a local corporation building in India with its red-brick walls and low-maintenance gardens. My perception changed the moment we stepped into the grand hall. It was decorated splendidly with idols, lamps and flowers in every corner. A pujari was reciting beautiful hymns. There was a massive and perfectly sculpted marble statue of Sai Baba at the other end of the room, which was adorned with jewels and a crown. The place smelled divine with many incense sticks burning in all corners. In a few minutes, when the hall was nearly packed with devotees, the *aarti* began, and everyone joined their hands, and the place went from beautiful to magical, from glorious to gloriously divine!

We took our prasad at the end of the aarti and walked out. 'Thanks for bringing me here,' Adira said as we waited for our Uber to take us back to the apartment.

I did not want the trip to end like that but failed miserably when it came to finding the right words, in the correct order, at the right time. Thankfully, while I was still battling with the words to form an excellent conversation starter in my head, Adira spoke. 'You are aware of my parents' circumstances, aren't you?'

I knew exactly what she was talking about. Her parents were in the process of getting divorced, and not many people knew about it. It all started when Adira moved out of Nani's house. Piyush had told me about the legal battle which involved a lot of money as Adira's parents were joint owners of a massive business empire. But I could not let her know or her trust on her best friend would be broken. It was Tamanna who had told Piyush, in confidence, who then told me, in good faith of course.

I shook my head, inviting her to tell me about it. I shall spare you the details of our emotional and lengthy conversation. What I will tell you is that we didn't take that particular Uber. Instead, we walked a little as she told me about her parents and their love which had got lost over the years, and I saw her in a new light. She had so much emotional baggage with her. We had a cup of coffee at a nearby cafe and later ate lunch at a restaurant. We returned to our respective rooms at 7 p.m.

That day, I knew things had changed. She saw me as someone she could trust, and I made a promise to myself to never break her trust at any cost. That was also the day when we held hands for the first time, and she rested her head on my shoulder—When? How? Why? As I said, I will spare you the details.

ALONE TIME . . . THAT WAS ALL I NEEDED

It had already been three weeks, and I had managed to go out alone with Adira only once. The entire group travelled together on weekends, as well as any weekday outings where Adira was mostly busy shopping, clicking pictures or having a gala time with her friends. Angad and Adira used to take a stroll together every evening though. And that didn't work well for me.

Why was I so insecure? Why couldn't I let her be with her men friends? To be honest, I do not, till today, believe that Angad wanted to be 'only friends' with her. I felt like this every time I saw them together and whenever our eyes met. Not mine and Adira's, I am talking about my eyes meeting Angad's eyes when we were around Adira. He gave me the looks that one only gives to one's enemy—a rival. I kind of liked the fact that he considered me a competitor; it was a great achievement for a boy like me, who, at one stage, could not even be considered an acquaintance of a girl like Adira.

Also, from Adira's point of view, I now understand how important her friends were for her. But back then, a small sense of insecurity crept up on me and irritated me until I saw them coming back from their leisurely walk, from my balcony (discreetly of course). I was happy to be spending my breaks at work with her, but I wanted to know exactly what she felt about me before we headed back to India. Rajbir and I spoke about her sometimes, and he always encouraged me to talk to her as much as I could.

~

I love the sight of the rising sun and my love for the view doesn't fade even during peak summers when some people cannot even bear to hear the word Sun. In Melbourne I woke up at three and went out to catch the morning sun once. The high-rise buildings were crowding the sky, making it impossible for anyone to get a glimpse of the sun in the most beautiful hour of the day. So, I took an Uber to Mt Ridley Road, an open space with nothing but nature. It was quite far from the city, but from what I had overheard from a colleague at work, 'It has the power to take your breath away'. It presented a contrast of low hills and valleys on one side and sky-high buildings on the other.

'Why are you up at such an ungodly hour in the morning?' my Bangladeshi Uber driver asked me jokingly as we neared my destination.

'I need some fresh air, and some time just for myself,' I told him 'and some time to think,' I thought.

We bid each other goodbye after an hour-long journey, and there I stood, all alone at a point from where the dim city lights were visible on my right, and the beautiful bronze sky was right in front of me. I saw the sunrise colour the dark sky in bright shades. It was a mesmerizingly beautiful sight. I just stood there marvelling at the beauty presented before me. Nothing remained—just nature and I. Suddenly the alarm on my phone beeped and bought me out of my thoughts or the absence of my thoughts- it was six thirty. I had been sitting there for almost two and a half hours! Not thinking about anything, in particular, just admiring nature but the beep reminded me that it was time to go back to my world. I closed my eyes to freeze the moment in my memories.

On my way back, I wished that someday, just someday I would come back there with Adira and I would sit holding hands as the Sun would rise up in the sky to witness our love.

On Friday, I walked into the office looking for an opportunity to ask her out, alone. During the lunch break, I found it difficult to eat the bland pasta. Adira and I had taken the same pasta from the cafeteria, and looking at her relishing her food made me question my taste buds. 'So . . . do you have . . . ahem . . . any plans for the evening?' I finally asked her, clearing my throat. I started toying with my food. That was all I could do with it—swirl it around the fork and pretend to be interested in it.

'No,' she replied carelessly, and smiled, stuffing her face with a forkful of salad. Over the weeks I had realized that it was easy for her to laugh and smile, but her smiles rarely reached her eyes, unlike during our college days. *Probably because of her parents' divorce,* I found myself thinking every time I saw her fail to smile like she used to. As Adira lifted her eyes from her plate to meet mine, I fell in love with her all over again, this time more hopelessly than ever because she looked at me as if she could read my thoughts—which was scary as hell but fascinating at the same time. I was getting caught in her web and drowning farther in her love, an inch farther every passing minute.

'Do you want to take a walk?' she asked me, and I became sure that somehow, she could indeed read my mind. *I need to think before I think in her presence,* I made a note in my head.

'We could walk up to the Yarra after work,' she recommended.

'I would love to,' I squeaked, and finally started eating my food. Nothing is bland or tasteless if there is happiness and hope in your heart, I realized.

~

'Aren't you late?' Adira's voice startled me as soon as I punched my identification card on the machine and stepped out of the office later that evening. I had been held back by Rajbir as he had caught me daydreaming during a session, and I had to redo the training with him. I had lost hope of going out with Adira that evening, but to my surprise, she'd waited for me after everyone left.

Dressed in a pair of black trousers and a white top, she was leaning against a brick wall with her hands in her pockets. Her oversized handbag hung over her right shoulder. She tilted her head a little and gave me a warm smile. Looking at her standing there, I grinned like a fool. 'Sorry,' I apologized, and we walked side by side towards the Yarra river.

It was time for almost everyone to head back home in CBD, and Adira and I became a part of the ever-swelling crowd as soon as we stepped out on the road. As we walked towards our destination, which was hardly a fifteen-minute walk from work, slowly and gradually, the crowd around us started thinning and finally vanished. We reached the bridge that connected the city from one side of the river to the other. As always, there were some tourists around, walking, laughing, creating memories and enjoying the view. Within fifteen minutes, we had escaped the madness of the busy world and entered a calm place where one could talk one's heart out.

We walked together in silence until Adira saw a modern art installation next to the bridge. 'Here, take my picture,' she ordered, handing me her phone, and dashed off to pose. The phone was locked.

'What is its password?' I asked her loudly.

'It is my birthday,' she said, and before she could add anything, '14 December' slipped out of my mouth. I bit my tongue. 'You remember my birthday? Only my mom remembers my birthday,' she said in excitement. 'I have a good memory,' I told her and regretted saying it within moments. 'Really? When is Piyush's birthday?' she quizzed me. I could have lied to her and got out of the situation but my mind works the least under pressure. 'Ammm . . . I don't know,' I told her with my cheeks on fire as I felt all the blood in my body rush towards my head. She didn't say anything, just gave me a sly smile for a while and then poked me with her elbow. I did not know what exactly did she think of me then, but I did know that we were on our way to becoming what I had always dreamt of us to be. I clicked a few pictures of her, she clicked a few of me, and we walked over to the bridge.

As Adira and I walked close to each other, without saying a word to each other, our hands brushed a few times and that made me nervous like a teenage boy. With my mind shut down due to the sudden contacts, I knew that restarting the conversation was out of scope so I decided to observe the beautiful scene in front of us instead. The Yarra looked so scenic and peaceful at that hour. The water was probably not the cleanest that I had seen, but it moved in a beautiful rhythm. It sparkled in the warmth of the sun. Trees on the other side swayed with the softly blowing breeze, a fading rainbow was visible in the distance, and the sweet sounds of twittering birds filled the space between us. People were rowing in the river. We leaned against the thick walls of the bridge. Adira placed her hand on the wall, and her beautiful bracelet shone like many diamonds. After what felt like hours Adira finally broke the silence, 'You have a good memory. Nowadays, who remembers birthdays?' she said.

I wondered how to answer, but I knew that I had to tell her now. I turned to face her. Her face looked exquisite in the twilight. Looking at her then, I understood how some women are beautiful in a way that can only be described through poems, not sentences; just verses. My inner voice said, *Ronnie, you might not get another chance; there will be no next time. It is either now or maybe never.*

I looked into her eyes. Sometimes a moment changes everything for you; it was that kind of moment for me. I realized that her happiness meant the world to me, and the look in her eyes gave me enough courage to conquer the world for her.

'Do you like your bracelet?' I asked her, and she looked at me as if she was asking herself, *Where is this going?*

'I do,' she replied, as if stating the obvious.

'I bought it for you,' I told her, and shrugged my shoulders when she gave me a sharp, surprised look. 'I couldn't tell you then because I was too shy to tell you that . . . that . . .' I added, and failed to finish the sentence.

'That?' she said with curiosity. I knew in my heart that she was aware of what was going to come out of my mouth next.

'That I wanted to be more than just friends with you,' I blurted out the words, keeping my eyes down. The words which had kept me awake at night for years were finally out there, between us, waiting for a response from her. I held my breath.

She was not angry with me, but she was not thrilled with my confession either. I had anticipated anger or happiness—but her slight indifference was beyond my understanding. 'You are a good guy, Raunak. I have known you for so long, and I like you, despite of not wanting to. I like you a lot,' she said, and looked at the bracelet. 'Love was not kind to me in the past. It took me months to rebuild myself. There was this man that my parents chose for me. I fell in love with him, and he threw me out of his life like garbage because he felt I was not good enough for him. For some people, love is not meant to be. I like you so much and love spending time with you, but I am not completely sure if I want to let anyone enter that corner of my heart ever again.' Her voice was low, and sadness filled her eyes.

I knew it would be hard for me to convince her for two reasons. First, she had suffered terrible heartbreak a few years ago, and second, her parents too had fallen out of love. It is easy to stop believing in the power of the most beautiful emotion mankind has ever known. But it is easier to quit; I was not going to quit. She liked me, and I was happy to wait until she was in love with me.

THINGS THAT HAD TO BE SAID

That evening when we came back, I skipped the team dinner and had my food alone in my room contemplating what to do next. It would be wrong to say that I was not angry with Adira. I was more than angry, and didn't want to face anyone. 'One heartbreak is not the end of your life!' I wanted to scream at her, 'Don't you see how much I love you?'

I decided to write her a few texts, but I wanted her to read them all before she sent me her response, or worse, blocked my number.

Finally, I found a solution—an email. Yes, the mode of communication which is the best for lovers after letters and calls, is email. Not many of us explore that option, but I feel that chatting or texting doesn't really convey our messages and tone well. I would prefer an email any day to a chat or text. I still have a copy of the email I wrote to her that evening. I didn't have her personal email id, so I sent it to her official email id instead, a stunt I would never recommend to anyone. I was a fool who played with his job. I could have been issued a warning. Or worse, I could have been terminated for the act. But a mind ruled by a heart drunk on love cannot understand any reasoning.

To: AdiraS@itcons.co.in
Bcc- ronniecool@gmail.com

Dear Adira,

Firstly, I want to apologize for sending this email to this email id, but I do not have your personal email id, and I didn't want to send a text as I feared you would block me before I'd said all that I want to.

Yes, it is true that I love you and I do not even know since when. But I am not asking you to like me back if you can't. All I am asking from you is a chance to see if we can be what I want us to be.

Whenever I see you, I feel all the love swelling inside deep within me and taking over all my senses. I know it sounds clichéd, but that is precisely what happens to me. Today, when we were walking together, it dawned on to me how much I wanted to be with you, more than I have ever wanted anything else in my life. Losing you to someone else would mean losing myself into a space too dark to imagine. I want anything but that.

All I can say to you is that just because of something which happened in the past, do not stop believing in love, do not stop looking for love, do not stop loving . . .

Raunak

I wrote and rewrote my name thrice with 'yours in love', 'always yours' before it, but then deleted all of that. Finally, I sent it with only my name. Just when I hit send, Rajbir walked into the room. I didn't want to meet his eye, so I covered myself with my blanket, pretending to be asleep.

Anyway, a response from Adira was not expected until the next morning, if she didn't walk straight to the HR department to get me terminated from my job.

A few minutes later there was a ping on my mobile phone. It was a message from her—she had read my email and wanted to talk.

'A phone call?' I asked her.

'Yes,' she replied to me, and I dialled her number as I walked into the living area. Thankfully, Rajbir was in the bathroom again, because I would have never called her in front of him.

'Hi,' Adira was talking in hushed tones, and I followed suit.

'Hi.'

'Listen, I want to tell you something before we do this,' I couldn't help but gape at her words. *Before we do this!*

'Yes . . . okay,' I managed to say. I was surprised and excited beyond words.

'Honestly, I didn't think that after failing in love once and seeing my parents' marriage fall apart in front of my eyes, I would dare to be in love again. I believed that love dies with time; it is an overrated emotion. Once it leaves your side, you are left alone. But it seems that I am still in love with the idea of love!' I heard a little smile at the end of her rather long sentence.

Sometimes I wonder if she and I were the same person. We were both a little broken, entirely messed up and madly in love with the idea of love.

'Love dies when you stop working on it,' I told her in a reassuring tone. My mind was running on an overdose of emotions.

I believe a man can easily fall for beauty, but external attraction doesn't last long. It is an intelligent mind that keeps anyone in love with their partner forever. When I say 'an intelligent mind', it doesn't mean that she had completed her college degree which is why she was smart, or that she could solve mathematical problems the fastest. It means a woman with whom I could have meaningful conversations all night long. Conversations that had the ability to make one go deeper into them; discussions that keep you up all night and give you goosebumps whenever you revisit them.

Our conversation that night was like that. I remember it word for word. We spoke about life—her life, and mine. Our goals, personal and otherwise, our emotional needs; and we discussed my favourite topic on earth—love.

'Love should make one breathless and weak. Love should allow one to let the other person into one's soul, with one's soul being a place which is so within me that I would change forever when love touches it!' Sometimes, even today I hear her words, as if she is whispering them to me, in my ears. I knew that I could move mountains for her if she would love me back. That was the first time she sang for me, on my insistence, of course. 'Tum pakar lo . . .' a song from an old Hindi movie, *Khamoshi*. Her voice gave me goosebumps, and the recollection of that time still does.

When she asked me to tell her something about me that no one else knows, I confessed to her that I loved photography and was planning to buy a professional DSLR camera. I told her that she had been my muse for the last three years and promised to send her a copy of all the pictures that I had taken of her as soon as we landed in India.

At 3 a.m., I realized that she had gone off to sleep as she'd stopped talking. I disconnected the call and slipped under my sheets, smiling like an idiot!

The next day, our team had plans to go to the Great Ocean Road. It was the last weekend before we went back home, and I was excited beyond words.

THE LAST NAIL IN THE COFFIN

When I woke up the next morning, I was not feeling very well. Rajbir checked my temperature which was slightly higher than normal, and I had a runny nose.

'We should cancel the outing,' Adira suggested when the rest of the team walked into the room to see how I was doing. I do not know how bad I actually looked, but judging by the look on everyone's faces, I think I looked way worse than I felt that day.

'But why?' Angad asked, surprising everyone. He looked at all the others in the room with his hands in the air. He was apparently not happy to miss out on his fun because of a measly-looking colleague who was sick.

'Angad is right. We should all go. This is our last chance to go out together, as a team, in Australia.' Rajbir was not too kind either. But I do not blame either of them as I would have reacted exactly the same way had Angad been down with a fever. *I wish that Angad gets the flu soon,* I slyly prayed.

'Will you be able to manage alone?' Adira asked, looking concerned, and I nodded, just to make her happy. Internally, I was dying and wanted someone to be by my side just in case.

'Have fun!' I managed to say as the team walked out. Both Adira and Angad turned around to give me a look before heading out.

I was alone and unwell. To add to my misery, Angad walked back in again. This time he was alone.

'I think she is not your type and you should step back,' he said, almost aggressively between clenched teeth. His eyes were cold as if he were threatening me. *Wait, he is threatening me!*

'What?' I attempted to get up from my bed, but failed. I seemed to be really weak. My reactions, which are usually quite slow, were the slowest they had ever been.

'Do not think you are fooling me. I know what you have been trying to do for the last few days. I can see what you feel for her, but trust me, she has no feelings for you or anyone for that matter, at this moment. She is a good friend of mine. I have known her for months now, and I can tell you that she is not very comfortable with your attempts to be all over her, so back off!' there was a severe warning in his tone. I could see that he was trying to mess things up.

'Really?' I faked a laugh, and ended up coughing like an old man. 'I have known her for far more years and months than you have. She is a grown-up girl who can speak her mind. If she has a problem with me or in being with me, she is very capable of telling me herself. You don't need to speak for her,' I growled at him, thanks to my sore throat, and before the unnecessary argument became more heated, I ducked my face under the duvet. *There is no point wasting your time on a conversation with an arsehole like him,* I told myself. My head was hurting as if it were going to burst with all the anger and rage in me, and to add to all that, there was this bloody Australian flu. Somehow, I always knew that Angad was trouble.

I had never been in a situation like this before, fighting over a girl with a man. *I think I should talk to Adira and tell her to put her friend in his place,* I decided, and dialled her number after I heard Angad stomp out of my room without closing the door behind him.

Surprisingly, Angad picked up my call. *What the . . .* words evaded me, and he didn't take long to say, 'I told you not to bother her.'

I decided to lie down and take a nap as I felt exhausted after the unwanted war of words.

Later, I lay in bed looking at the white ceiling above my head. The fever, as well as Angad's words, had hit me hard. *It is evident that she doesn't want you to bother her. She did not even pick up your call.* That was true, but it was also true that we had had such a fantastic time together; we had had such nice conversations, and she trusted me enough to tell me about her parents. Even that morning when she'd spoken to me, she'd sounded so concerned. It was not adding up. If everything was actually as good as I thought, then why had she not taken my call? Why did she allow Angad to talk to me? My own thoughts and Angad's words kept rushing through my brain. I recall waking up a few times with disturbing thoughts about Adira and Angad in my head. *Adira will enjoy her day in my absence with Angad . . .* I was being as melodramatic as a Hindi film actress. I was the good guy in our love story but failed miserably when a surge of anger filled my heart. No thoughts, rational or otherwise, came to me. I was thoughtless and blank for the first time in ages. I could think of nothing, and soon I drifted into the world of nightmares.

When I woke up, I was feeling much better—physically. The fever was gone. I could tell that without the aid of a thermometer. I felt lighter in the head as the throbbing pain was gone, even though my nose was still blocked, and my throat hurt as if someone had mowed it using a tiny lawnmower.

I adjusted my pillows to sit up, and did what anyone does once they wake up—I aimlessly scrolled on my phone. It was not connected to the hotel Wi-Fi, so I had nothing new to look at. I plugged my phone into free data and went into the loo while it synced. When I came back, to my surprise, there were a few WhatsApp calls as well as messages on the phone—mostly from Adira and Rajbir.

I responded to Rajbir's messages to let him know that I was feeling much better and was happy that they were enjoying their trip. Adira too had asked me if I was okay, but I chose to ignore her courtesy texts. After my heated conversation with Angad last evening, I needed time to figure out where it was all going, and honestly, I had entirely convinced myself that she was toying with my heart and feelings. My ego, which I believed I termed as self-respect then, raised its ugly head from under all the love that I had for her and ruled my actions.

More than Angad, I was angry and upset with Adira. She had made me believe that she felt something for me. We were friends, and she could have told me directly if she was not interested. *I never crossed my limits. Who is Angad? Why had she involved him?* I recall saying such things to myself all day while analysing and overanalysing the situation. The rational 'me' should have just waited for them to return and talked to Adira about what had happened between Angad and me. But the rational 'me' was not well, and the new me was high on ego, the worst of human emotions. I decided to overthink and make matters worse. I was only interested in shutting her out of my life and forgetting the last three years of my life which I had mostly spent thinking about Adira. It is never easy to forget the first love of your life, even if it is a one-sided love affair; all the memories come back to haunt you, all night, every night. But I had to try no matter how difficult it was.

This was the beginning of a new phase in my life, the worst period in a way.

I slept in all day on Sunday as well despite feeling much better. I had neither the company nor the will to go out and explore or enjoy my last day in Australia. I packed my bags and ate all three meals in the hotel room watching old Hindi movies on Netflix and crying. I am not someone who cries at the drop of a hat, but that Sunday was one of my few weak days. I felt alone and very lonely. I called my parents who were attending a family wedding, and the feeling of being ignored by them made matters worse. My sister was somewhere at a doctor's clinic in London and was too busy to take my call. She was not unwell as my mother later told me. She just had to visit a doctor that day for a regular check-up.

Finally, at around 9 p.m., the group returned from their second outing. It was still quite bright outside, as in Melbourne the sun sets around 10 p.m. in the summer. I heard their happy banter and laughter through the walls of the corridor and felt sick in the stomach again. I could hear Angad's voice followed by Adira's laughter. The noises brought more tears to my eyes. For some unknown reason, I felt that I shouldn't see Adira ever again. She had said nothing to me, and had done nothing wrong either. In fact, she had been the nicest to me in the past few days, and things were exactly as I had wanted them to be. It was Angad who had planted the seeds of jealousy and made me feel betrayed. The feeling was not going to let go of me so quickly or easily.

We had an early morning flight at 7 a.m. the next day. *Cry all you want tonight as tomorrow will be a new day*, I promised myself, and covered my face with my duvet the moment I heard Rajbir's footsteps inside the apartment. My luggage was stacked in the living area. Rajbir called out my name a few times. When I didn't respond, he gave up and started packing his own bags. Half an hour later, all the commotion died down, and the only noise that remained was Rajbir's soft snores.

MY HOME, NEW DELHI

THREE DAYS LATER

I had finally completely recovered from the flu and was to join work the next Wednesday. That gave me a few more days to relax, but typically, I utilized the next few days in overthinking and ensuring that my mind did not go back to its normal rational state. Physically, I was much better than when I left Melbourne, but mentally I think I was at the lowest I had ever been in my life. My uneasiness did not go unnoticed, even though I wanted it to. My mother, who like all the other mothers in the world has hawk-eyed vision, figured out that something was extremely wrong but couldn't put her finger on exactly what was troubling her child. She had been worried about me ever since I'd come back home and had been trying to guess the reasons, primarily focusing on flus of all kinds known to man.

'You have come back with some foreign flu which is not going away. You must get yourself checked for swine flu as well as bird flu. I have asked your papa to check with Doctor Mehra if it could be Ebola,' my melodramatic mother said with tears in her eyes. That was the moment

I figured out where I'd got my overthinking, my over-worrying nature from—it was all in the genes.

'Relax, Mummy. It is nothing. Moreover, I feel much better today compared to the first day in Melbourne. All I have now is a bit of cold. It will go on its own in a few days' time,' I tried my best to reassure her, but she was not the type to be easily convinced. Thankfully, she had not discovered Doctor Google then, or she would have declared that I had cancer of some kind for sure.

I had last seen Adira at the Indira Gandhi International Airport where our flight had landed three days ago. Thankfully, I was given a seat next to a stranger on the long, exhausting sixteen-hour flight. I was glad to have some comparatively warmer Indian food, which the flight attendant on our Air India flight served smilingly. Despite being unwell as well as heartbroken, I was delighted and relieved to be going back, to my people, my country, my home. I slept through most of the flight as there was no point in hurting myself looking at Adira and Angad sitting close together in the seats opposite mine, watching movies and laughing. My only interaction with Adira throughout that day was when we had first entered the airport. She asked me why I had not replied to any of her calls or texts the day before. 'I was and am unwell,' I told her without looking at her.

'Come, Adira,' I heard Angad call her, and she walked away from me. From her expression, it was evident that she was hurt with the way I responded to her, but I was protecting myself and my heart. I saw her go and join her friends, and I closed my eyes to hide my pain and strengthened my resolve. I had to get over her.

It was unlike me, but my thoughts didn't take a break, even on the flight. I recalled how the last few days had brought us together in an inexplicable way. I saw it as the beginning of love, but it was most definitely not the way Adira saw it, or that was what I believed then. I had decided that she looked at me purely as a friend. All she wanted was friendship, and all she was ready to give was friendship. When she spoke to me openly about her feelings, when she held my hand in the cab, when she placed her hand on my shoulder, I had started building my dream castle, slowly and steadily, while for her these were clearly only friendly gestures.

I had wanted more, but she had placed me in her friend bucket. *I was lying in that bucket, struggling to get out and attract her attention. I was trying to get annoyingly close to her. I felt disgusted every time I recalled the fact that she did not tell me on her own that she wanted me to back off. Instead, she assigned the job to someone else. Maybe because she thought of it as a waste of time—that I was a waste of her time!* Negative thoughts with no solid foundation sprout in my brain at the slightest of provocation. While it takes me ages to find positive thoughts and convince them to make my head their home, negative thoughts seldom need an invite.

After skipping more than a few get-togethers at my cousin's house, I finally gave in to my mother's request of accompanying her to a Sangeet ceremony. It was one day before I was to go back to work and meet Adira, pretending that nothing had happened. I had been ignoring my mother's pleas and avoiding meeting anyone, but it was about time I came out of my self-created gloom. So, I agreed and saw my mother's spirits lift. She had some plans for me—a surprise as she put it. I almost knew I was in for a shock later that evening.

Most of what happened that day is a blur in my memory, maybe because nothing significant had happened in my life since my brawl with Angad. In the evening, I accompanied my mother and met a lot of my cousins and distant relatives.

There was a lot of noise, chaos and irritatingly happy vibes at the Sangeet ceremony. Everyone was happy about someone else getting married, and I was probably unhappy because they were not focusing on me. In a Punjabi family, a relative who has returned from abroad is the centre of attention, although things are changing a little now as more and more people travel internationally, courtesy of their companies. Families now regard the ones who are either permanently settled abroad or are there for their studies as more important. Foreign returns like me were plentiful in all families, and we were considered second-class citizens compared to our NRI relatives.

At this point, I think it is important for me to recount what happened earlier that evening. We are a big family, and more than a few of my cousins, including both close and distant ones, get married every year. Around the time when the marriage season is in full swing, we hardly ever stay at home, any evening. There is always a function to attend. While Dad and I need only a few minutes to get dressed, Mummy begins her ritual in the afternoon for an evening get-together. My dad and I never disturb her, and I assumed that the same protocol would be followed that evening too. But to my surprise, my mother spent most of her time that evening in my room, selecting and rejecting clothes for me to wear for the function. 'I do not think anyone cares about what I wear, Mummy. I only go to parties to stuff myself with good food,' I told her, shamelessly grinning at my own joke, for the first time in many days.

'Here, try this combination,' she handed me a white shirt, beige trousers and a black jacket. I took the clothes from her and went into the bathroom to change. I could not help but overhear my mother talking to someone on the phone while I was getting dressed.

'Yes, he is. He just returned from Australia,' I heard her say. *Bragging to someone over the phone. Oh, how much I love my mother.* She was so proud of me while we were at home. But her mood changed as soon as we entered the wedding venue and were greeted by the laughter coming from the end where my NRI cousin was playing a flute.

'I should have worn my black trousers with this blazer,' I told my mother, trying to take her mind off the unnecessary stress she felt as my cousin basked in the limelight.

'No, you look just fine,' Mummy replied, without taking her eyes off the group standing around the NRI admiring the funny tune he played.

However, it did not take long for her to come out of her sad state. Soon her kitty party group was bored, and all of them gathered together to discuss the important stuff—the food at the party—and Mummy delightedly joined them, but not before issuing her instructions to me.

'Be around and answer your phone when I call you,' she told me and I nodded my head before leaving her with the group.

After wandering around for a few minutes, I parked myself close to the dance floor, in the middle of the closed banquet hall. Very loud music played. I was thankful that I was unable to hear anything or anyone. It was the perfect place for me to stand and watch as people passed by. Some were dancing, some drinking, some doing both. Amidst the music and lights, memories of Adira managed to creep back into my head.

I got some time to reflect upon what had happened those last few days in Australia. I could see that I was probably overreacting. Angad could just be a jealous friend who wanted me to stay away from Adira, and he had planted all this in my head, with my help of course. Maybe Adira had nothing to do with any of this. The more I thought about it, the more I saw things in a different light. I was finally looking beyond what Angad had made me see, and I realized how shallow I had been because of that one jealous moment when Angad said something. *All it took was a few words to forget all that Adira and you had built*—I wondered why. I always wanted to be with her, even when she didn't know my name, and now when there was a chance, I had blocked her out of my life. Maybe it was fear of some sort. Maybe I thought that she was too good for me, and that I was not perfect for her. Probably, I was worried about losing her before I'd even had the chance to get her.

I had ignored her texts and phone call when they were at the Great Ocean Road, and I'd ignored her completely on the flight. I had to be brave and talk this out with her. I realized that so far it had been the totally wrong way to approach the situation. I needed to act maturely. *Better late than never,* I told myself.

Standing there, in the middle of the crowd, I could think better than I'd done sitting alone in my room. Despite all the noise that surrounded me, I could hear the pleas of my heart better than I had in the silence of my own space. It took me a split second to fish out my mobile phone from my pocket and type a message to her.

Two hours went by very painfully as all I did was look at my phone which stared back at me in disappointment. *Call her,* I knew it made sense. So, I found my way out of the chaos to call and maybe apologize to her. I called her number, and surprisingly, her phone was switched off. I wondered what had happened. *Maybe she has blocked you*, I really needed to watch my thoughts—they were my real enemy at times.

I took a cousin's phone and dialled her number just to check if what I thought was true. Thankfully it wasn't. Her phone was actually switched off, though I would have preferred to talk to her and find out why she had blocked my number instead. At least that meant all was well with her, and my worries could take a break.

As I was returning and thanking my cousin for lending me phone, I saw my mother stomping over to us. The look on her face was full of anger and irritation, and I guessed it had something to do with the NRIs. Unfortunately, it didn't. Somehow, I had managed to miss three of her phone calls, and she was there to scold me in front of everyone without considering the fact that I was no longer a kindergarten student—typical of my mom.

Once her lecture on how careless and reckless I am was over, she came closer to me and screamed with all her force into my ears, 'Chalo, I want you to meet someone.'

'Who?' I asked her, but the music was still on, and people on the dance floor were crazily screaming as well, which meant that my voice was lost in the melee. I wondered who was going to meet me there and get bored listening to all of my achievements, primarily my work (which no one understood) and the fact that I had just returned from Australia, as there was hardly anyone at the party whom I did not know already.

Mummy held my hand tightly, and we walked towards a table in the corner of the hall. Two pretty girls and three middle-aged women sat at the table full of food and drinks. Thankfully, the music was not as loud around that table, and none of us had to shout our greetings to one another.

'This is your Seema aunty. You remember her, don't you?' my mother gestured towards the lady sitting next to the two girls. Honestly, I didn't know her, but I did know the drill to be followed whenever I met a 'your' aunty. I was supposed to bend down and touch the lady's feet, and smile at her as if we have known each other for ages. She would pat my back or hit me on my head, or worse, kiss me on my cheek, tattooing me with her red lips. I did exactly what was expected and repeated the drill two more times for the other two ladies at the table who were 'my' Seema aunty's sisters. All three of them patted my back, and I was finally allowed to take a seat.

By now I knew I was being introduced to girls for an arranged match. People think that usually only girls in India are nagged, blackmailed and sometimes even forced to get married after they attain a certain age. Well, boys too are often not spared. They too are blackmailed, taunted or forced when it comes to getting married. The day I got my first job appointment letter, my mother started looking for excuses to tell me that I shouldn't wait forever to get married, and then a few evenings later, the torturous rounds of arranged-marriage meetings began.

'And this is Bhavna,' my mother introduced me to one of the girls, who was looking as disinterested in meeting me as I was in her. With our respective mothers around, we extended our hands for a formal hello, and then busied ourselves with our phones—mindlessly scrolling, to be specific. Our mothers too began with stupid, aimless work banter about whose kid was better and why they were the better party if a match were to take place.

Fifteen minutes later, I finally raised my eyes from the screen. Not that anyone had asked me to—I had run out of scrolling options after a session on Facebook, Instagram,

Twitter, YouTube and then back to Facebook. I looked at the faces of all the females around me. I realized that the younger women looked like the same person dressed in different clothes—*Twins probably,* I concluded unnecessarily. My mother realized that I was back in the meeting and began probing Bhavna, 'So beta, tell us about your workplace.'

Resting her hands on her lap, the girl began a pre-rehearsed introduction to her work. The only thing I heard was that she was working in a bank near my office. Thereafter, I lost her, and my mind drifted back to Melbourne. Sometime later, when I came back to their discussion, I heard Bhavna's mother merrily listing some facts about her daughter while trying to arrange another meeting, '. . . Bhavna is a great cook. Why don't you guys plan a lunch with us the coming Sunday? You can meet Bhavna's father too . . .'

I couldn't take the yo-yo of thoughts any more, and I was well aware that sitting there would do me no good. So, I politely excused myself from the party and walked away, even though I felt my mother's glare almost burn my back as I headed towards the exit. It was the only place where there was less noise. My mind was empty as I waited for my mother for what felt like an eternity. I knew she would follow me there. I was done for the day. I had had enough food, met many of my cousins, heard all about prospective brides, had been glared at by my mother more than enough times, was tired and had to return to work the next day. I explained all this to Mummy, who had nothing to say and agreed to head back. Dad had already gone back home with Rohit like he usually did at family gatherings—his fake headache always appeared magically at around 9 p.m., and Rohit was ready, as always, with his bike, at his beck and call. By 10 p.m. Dad is tucked in his bed and snoring.

On our way back, Mummy told me how she thought that I would soon be past my sell-by date in the wedding market. 'You have just returned from abroad and will get the best matches right now. It is now or never. If we miss this chance, you will have to settle for a less-than-ordinary wife.' I wanted to remind her that I was not beyond 'ordinary' myself, so how and why does she expect an above-average bride for me? But then Adira is not ordinary or average; she is way out of my league. But why do we have these leagues in the first place? Why are these leagues based on looks? I could not disagree with and hate the grading system more than I did when I realized how important it was for everyone, including my own mother.

Back home, Bhavna and her mother were all that my mother could talk about as she prepared midnight tea for both of us. I couldn't sleep and kept dialling and redialling Adira's number, and Mummy couldn't sleep with all the excitement after meeting her future daughter-in-law. I was sure she was going to dream about future kids that night!

Who have you been calling?' she couldn't help asking after my hundredth attempt to call Adira.

'No one . . . Rohit, actually . . .' I lied, and bit my tongue. I hated lying to my mother but how could I tell her that I was obsessing about the whereabouts of a girl I had a nameless relationship with.

'Talk to me then,' she said, looking at me. I was supposed to put my phone away at this point. 'Seema Aunty wants to talk to you,' she said, holding my hand tightly as she started talking again.

'I do not remember Seema Aunty or her sister, Mummy. What will I talk to her about?' I asked her honestly. 'Have I even met her before?'

'You are right; you have never met her before, but that does not matter,' she said, giggling. She started to tell me about this new Seema aunty.

'Okay, so Seema is the wife of Dr Chadda, the vet in Amar Colony who had this huge bungalow in the lane next to Nani's house. The yellow one. Do you recall seeing it?'

I knew the place she was talking about, although I still could not figure out who these people were. But at this point, I was very far from saying no to her. 'Yes, I have,' I lied.

She continued, 'Nani told her about your big job when you were in Australia, and we are trying to fix you up with Bhavna . . .'

By the time I went to my room, I was happy with myself as a son. Mummy and I had had a good conversation. Sometimes in life, you do not need big words of wisdom to clear your head; sometimes all you need is a cup of tea with your mother who would talk endlessly about things that don't matter to you, but seeing her happy, smiling and excited takes away all the stress and uncertainty of the future. My situation with Adira was still the same, but I was not thinking the worst any more. I picked up a pen and opened the notepad in front of me to scribble my thoughts before hitting the sack. It was a long-lost habit.

The next day I woke up with the same words inside my head that I had etched on the paper the night before:

> 'Love filled a space in my heart, a space which I did not know even existed. It was like a serene sunset. I was mesmerized beyond words by it before it left me alone in the darkness.'

NEXT DAY AT WORK

I was late, which was not unusual. I had hardly slept the previous night, so it was nearly impossible for me to arrive on time, and I reached the office at 10.30 a.m. sharp, precisely an hour late. I expected the entire team to be at work and planned to talk to Adira during the break to clear the air.

Everyone was at their desks, sitting and pretending to work except Adira. She didn't seem to be in. I occupied my seat and started my pretence. A few months into the job, I had mastered the art. I thought of asking Rajbir about Adira's absence but as luck would have it, Rajbir too was busy the entire day. He had back-to-back meetings, and it didn't look right to invade the only breathing space that he had during his lunch hour for a personal inquiry. But I had to know, so I decided to talk to Prateek, another senior guy in the administration team, who was in charge of attendance. My luck never favours me, and that day was no exception. Prateek was also not available since he was working from home.

I did not know who else to ask about Adira's whereabouts but resolved not to think the worst and kept trying her number. I had to wait until the next day for a meeting with Prateek, so most of my first day back at work was spent worrying about Adira. I wrote and rewrote a report three times before getting it right and sending it to the client, only to realize that I had sent the email to a wrong email id, such was my state of mind.

At around 5 p.m., luckily, I spotted Sakshi, Adira's friend, strolling towards the pantry for a coffee break. I followed her in there like a puppy.

'Sakshi!' I called her name a little too loudly. Three other girls turned their heads towards me and laughed in unison. Lowering my head to hide my embarrassment, I walked towards Sakshi and smiled to initiate a conversation. I had hardly spoken to her at work since we had become team members or during our stay in Melbourne. Now when I think of it, I know why Sakshi's face had a *Why are you talking to me?* look when I inquired about her life.

'So, where is Adira?' I finally managed to ask when I realized that she was already bored of the conversation and had started fidgeting with her phone. It was an indication that the conversation was about to end, and so was her break.

'I am not sure, yaar. Her phone is switched off. I thought you might know. She did not even turn up for Angad's birthday last night when we had made plans to party at . . .' Sakshi had a story to tell, but her audience was not interested in knowing the details of Angad's birthday. So I interrupted her abruptly and shamelessly, something I am not very proud of. 'Oh, okay, I am not on a break. I shall talk to you about his birthday during my break,' I lied to her, not that she seemed to mind. She was a busy girl, and she got a call at the same moment as I headed back to my seat.

It was a painful night, but like all things it too passed. The next day as soon as I reached work, I paid my visit to Prateek's desk.

'I know her phone is switched off,' he told me in a calm tone when I worriedly informed him that a team member, who lived alone in the big city, was missing and no one had seen or spoken to her since we came back. 'She did not do the right thing by vanishing like this. I tried to call her as soon as I got to know from Rajbir,' he added.

'What did she not do right?' I asked him. To my surprise, he paused to check his emails. How could he tell me only half of the information, that too like a riddle, get then continue his work!

'Oh, I thought you knew! Adira has resigned.' He told me, shrugging his shoulders. His eyes were still glued to his laptop screen.

I did not prolong our conversation. I thanked him, and then with all my effort, I dragged my feet back to my work desk, where I was supposed to be all this time. *She'd resigned!* Finally, I let the words out with a gush of air. To say that I was shocked is an understatement—my world had turned upside down.

It took a while for it to sink in that Adira had resigned and had cut off all her colleagues from her life, including me. *So, no matter what you thought, you were just a colleague for her.* The obvious played in my mind on a repeat mode all day. That explained why she did not even bother to reply to my messages on Facebook.

So there I was, worried sick and fearing the worst, all last night and the night before. I had prayed hard that all the evil thoughts which had managed to find their way into my head were untrue. There are very few times in my life when I have wiped the tears from the corners of my eyes in for someone other than myself, but that night, with my mind on an overdose of emotions, more than a few tears trickled down and found their way on to my cheeks and then my pillow.

But the good news was that she was well, merrily enjoying her life somewhere with new people, new colleagues maybe. I was exactly where I had always been—more in love with her than ever now, after knowing her in the past three weeks. That evening, after bolting the doors of my room at night, I scribbled one line on my diary-:

> She is gone, again and again, and I failed to tell her how much I loved her . . .

ONE MONTH LATER

An orderly life followed in the next thirty-odd days—home-office-home. Nothing worth mentioning happened apart from one message from Adira on Facebook to tell me that she was okay and had gone back to live with her mother in Chandigarh. She had also mentioned that she was looking forward to spending some time away from social media. It was more of an informative, generic message she sent to all her friends who were worried sick about her, like me.

After receiving her message, I did not even reply to acknowledge that I had received it. But as hopeless as I was, I logged in to Facebook just a few days later to see if she was online and could talk a little. Surprisingly, she had even deactivated her Facebook account. I followed suit and deactivated mine too. After all, I had made the account only for her. I resolved not to bother her if she did not wish to talk to me.

It was very tough for me to forget her, to forget all that we had, to forget all that we could have had; had she given us a chance to explore the possibilities. At that point, I was convinced that I was not entirely at fault, although maybe I was partially responsible for what happened between us in Melbourne on our last day there. The rest of the responsibility lay with Adira—those were the thoughts in my mind then.

While I was broken and shaken from within, I threw myself into my office work, so that any time of the day, I had nothing else to think about; this was a deliberate attempt to stay sane. My bosses were impressed with me, or so I was told at the end of every week by Rajbir, and I had no reason not to believe him. He even gave me hints that I was most likely due for a promotion shortly, which meant a better pay cheque would come my way soon. Both my parents were beyond elated when I broke the good news to them. As I had expected, my darling mother spread the story of an impending promotion like wildfire in her social circle, and we started receiving more than the usual number of dinner invites.

How was I feeling? I don't know how to answer that.

Honestly, I didn't care a dime about the promotion or appraisals, or about the evaluations or reports that I worked on so diligently all through the day. They were mere distractions—I was distracting myself as I didn't want to do something stupid again and make myself look like a desperate fool in front of Adira. My attempts bore fruit during the morning hours. I hardly had more than a couple of passing thoughts that reminded me of her. It was the nights which brought with them fond memories; the hours had started to scare me.

I usually reached home at around 11 p.m., with an exhausted body which had to be dragged to the bedroom after a quick dinner at the table with Mother. She looked worried about me. 'Is everything all right?' she had asked me a few times during those awkward silences, and I blamed my lack of energy and enthusiasm on my great job and the workload it brought with it. 'There is no need to work this hard, you know,' she always suggested with a concerned look in her eyes. I knew that she knew it was not just work that was exhausting me and eating my soul.

Every single night, as soon as I stepped into my bedroom and switched off the lights to get some rest, sadness overpowered tiredness. From the time my head hit the pillow till the time I painfully drifted off to sleep everything that we had done together in Australia, every moment spent in each other's company haunted me. I wondered how she was and if she missed me even a bit.

I knew that she didn't at all feel the way I felt for her. Not even for a moment were we on the same page emotionally. For if she had even once felt these emotions as strongly as I did, she would not have just turned her back on me like this. Walking away from the person one has a special bond with, without even once looking back to see if they survived the unexpected blow of your exit, is something that no human, no matter how strong they are, can do. Such were the thoughts that kept me tossing and turning in my bed for many hours. Like clockwork, days and nights passed, but nothing changed.

I tried to bleed on my diary, but the most persuasive words and the harshest of thoughts came to me whenever I decided to write. Writing them down made me sink deeper into gloom. I was in an emotional zone which was making me hollow from within.

'Your eyes are losing their spark,' Rajbir pointed out to me once when we were on a tea break together. I ignored his remark and avoided meeting his eyes for many days. He must have guessed what I was going through, but I had no intention of discussing my heartbreak with anyone at work.

He should not be bothering about my 'spark' as long as his work is getting done on time, every time, I thought angrily before I fell asleep. In short, I had started hating almost everyone around me.

Adding to my pain, Rohit had met a girl whom he called 'the girl of his dreams'. 'Cheesy,' I said to his face when he told me excitedly, and I witnessed all his excitement melt away. He had been dating her for quite a while then and they eventually became each other's happily ever after, but that is another story. Now, I am happy for them. Back in those days, I hated her for snatching away my best friend at the time when I needed him the most. The mere mention of her name spoilt my mood. I had turned into a selfish moron, to say the least—and I know that, now. But my situation was as it was; Rohit was my best pal, and I could see Sagarika as nothing less than the devil personified.

A month of sadness ended when, out of nowhere, I received a text from Piyush with Adira's new number. It was a cold, breezy evening, and I was out with my family for a picnic at India Gate. While my mother was arranging a plastic mat and Dad was following her instructions on what to take out from the basket next and where to keep it, I sneaked away just far enough so they could not hear me talk on the phone, but I could still see them. I took a deep breath and dialled Adira's new mobile number with nothing specific in my mind. Actually, my thoughts were running like a freight train—there was so much to say; so much to ask for; so much to listen to; but I wanted to act cool, and not let her realize how much she had hurt me without even knowing, and how badly I wanted to hear her voice. So, I decided to generally chit-chat with her and ask her about her present situation. *Do not talk about the past*, my mind repeated again and again as the phone rang. I could feel my heart racing.

She did not answer the call then but ten minutes later, there was a message from her to say that she would call back—a promise which she never fulfilled.

'Stupid!' I screamed aloud, and Mummy looked at me with her eyes wide and her mouth gaping open.

'Why are you screaming? And whom are you screaming at?' my mother scolded me, and I swiftly apologized to her. In our house, only my mummy could scream, that too at my father or me.

I was losing my grip on my emotions. I knew that calling her had been a bad idea. After all, she had not shared her new number with me on her own. She wanted me to stay away, but I was behaving like a roadside Romeo.

That evening, I revisited the pages of my diary and traced a few words which I had written out of desperation, a few days ago.

You and I, I and You—we lived, we laughed, we loved, but we could never be 'we' because we were—I and You.

I turned the page over; the ink had marked the same words on the next page too. The words stared into my soul, there was no escaping them—I could not escape the emptiness.

13 FEBRUARY 2018

The day had finally arrived when the lovebirds, Piyush and Tamanna, were getting married. We were all happy for them; some were even relieved that the saga was going to enter a new phase. From the day their marriage card arrived at our house, Mummy declared that I was officially late as per the general marriage standards. 'Who are these people who decide who is late and who is early? Don't they have some better work to do?' Mummy's declaration triggered my already-loaded gun of anger and frustration, and I was unstoppable. I said things which I shouldn't have. Mummy replied to the initial few questions I screamed at her, and then she ignored the rest of my rant. She figured out that I had lost my mind and was not to be messed with. I want to apologize to my parents too through this book, for all the wrongs that I did during that phase, and afterwards: my unruly tone, my mood swings, the taunts, ignoring them—everything. And I want to thank them for being so supportive despite being unaware of the reason why I was behaving the way I was. I love them. Mummy and Papa—I love you.

Coming back to Piyush's wedding, his parents behaved as if their son were the first-ever boy to get married on this planet. No expense was spared; no opportunity to spend money was missed. Their wedding rituals and functions were to last for seven long days, and six of my evenings had already been spent in the lovely company of my family and cousins. It was the last day; the wedding ceremony was to take place at Tivoli Garden, Chhattarpur.

Rohit had introduced his new girlfriend to his family, and they had been attending all the family functions together as a couple. We had hardly had a proper conversation with each other in days as I was behaving like his jealous ex-girlfriend. Every time Rohit approached me, I turned my back and walked away. It did not end there. Every time his girlfriend, Sagarika, saw me, I gave her the most disgusted look, and she immediately backed away.

Why was I so grumpy, sad and annoying? It had been months since Adira had left. Initially, I did not want to talk about everything that had happened between us. That was when everyone was interested in knowing what was wrong with me. Now, when I was looking for someone to talk to, everyone had suddenly decided to accept my behaviour as it was and get on with their lives; like I didn't matter. Silly as it may sound, I was more upset over this than I was upset about Adira.

With no one else to talk to, I approached the groom. 'Is Adira coming?' I had asked Piyush quite casually a day before the wedding. I had not spotted her when we went to Tamanna's house to give Sagan—a ritual where the groom's family brings gifts for the bride. It is supposed to be a quiet affair with only the immediate families present, but Punjabis make it as grand as it can get with a minimum of 100 guests.

'Tamanna wanted her to attend the wedding so much. They are best friends, you know. We went to her mother's house in Chandigarh to invite them as well. Let's see if she decides to show up at all. Tamanna will be heartbroken if she doesn't come . . .' he shrugged his shoulders and replied. I could feel his eyes on me, but I dared not meet them. Despite all the time which had passed, I could not make myself move on. Thoughts of Adira still dominated my nights, and it was getting tough to fully occupy my days to keep my memories from invading my mind.

'Ufff! Why are you not dressed yet? We need to meet a family before the *varmala* happens, as after that there is just too much noise, and one can hardly hear anything,' my mother interrupted my thoughts, and started helping me with my blue necktie. It has always been tricky for me to tie a tie. I had learnt it in school but could never manage the perfect knot which other kids boasted of by opening the tie with a single pull. Mummy tied it effortlessly and gave me a satisfied smile as I pulled it up to my collar. 'You look quite good today,' she complimented me, and finally left me alone to put my shoes on.

'I am ready,' I said, walking out of the door. Both my parents were looking their best and so was I—I think. They waited for me in the dining area. Papa tossed his car keys at me. I was always the chauffeur at family functions—a role I did not mind taking up since Papa usually drank a little too much for everyone's safety and could not be trusted. That evening he was half a bottle down even before he was in his party clothes. Why? A family member getting married was reason enough to go to a place already tipsy.

Thanks to the horrendous traffic and many other wedding parties interrupting our way, we reached Tivoli Garden on Punjabi time, two hours after the time given to the bride's family. Surprisingly, we were pretty much the best performers when it came to timelines. We were definitely better than most at 90 per cent of the wedding parties we attended.

As always, just outside the wedding hall the groom's party decided to make an endlessly long haul and danced like there was no tomorrow. Coins were thrown in the air for the bandsmen to pick up—this was done to avoid the evil eye.

Fifteen minutes later, Mummy decided that it was all too exhausting for her and we could not step into the banquet hall with the rest of our party; we had to go in immediately. She held my hand and dragged me out of the Nagin dance challenge amongst cousins, which was being judged by the groom sitting in his carriage.

'Aunty Ji, let the groom cut the ribbon first, and only then we will let you guys in,' Piyush's pretty sisters-in-law protested.

'That is not needed,' Mummy declared, and held the delicate red ribbon in her hand. The girls looked at her in horror, fearing that she might rip the ribbon off. I heard them all breathe a sigh of relief when Mummy lifted up the fabric and made space for us to pass under it.

That's my mother for you—I wanted to say out loud but did not. I grinned at my mother, who followed no rules, ever. We heard the group of girls mumble as we passed them, but there was little me or Dad could do about it. Once Mummy puts her mind to something, nobody and nothing can stop her.

As expected, a girl and her family sat in the centre as we arrived. Honestly, she was the best-looking girl I had met so far in an arranged match. She had a sweet smile and lovely dark eyes. Like a ritual, my mother first talked to the girl's family about some random stuff and then started questioning the girl. I was asked similar questions by the girl's father and brother. I had become a pro at the wedding questionnaire and could almost predict the questions even before they were thrown my way:

'Where is your office located?'

'How much do you earn every month?'

'Is there a chance that you might think of settling abroad? Canada, maybe?'

'Will you mind if she works or doesn't work after marriage?'

Blah blah blah . . .

We sat chit-chatting until the ribbon was finally cut and everyone else walked in. Piyush's sisters-in-law earned a little over Rs 50,000 that evening for the task.

'I want to see them exchange the garlands,' I declared, and excused myself from the table. The ladies, including my mother, muttered behind my back as I walked away from them.

Piyush, all my cousins and their friends stood on the beautifully decorated stage. A couple of mighty chairs were placed on it for the bride and groom to sit while the photographers got to work. The set-up was just like any other wedding, yet I knew that by now the ladies would have figured out the good and the bad things about the stage decoration, the bride and groom's attires and the music and made mental notes. These notes would be revisited at every other kitty party for the next many weeks.

After approximately fifteen minutes, the DJ, who had been playing peppy Punjabi numbers, switched to an old Hindi film song and announced that the bride was to enter. All eyes were fixed on the main gate, and mine were no exception—even though my reason for looking in that direction was completely different. While everyone wanted to get a glimpse of the beautiful bride, I could not kill the small flicker of hope in my heart. *She might accompany Tamanna to the stage*, my love-infested mind hoped, and my eyes forgot to blink as my heart raced faster than Piyush's—this is an assumption though, based on no facts or data.

Suddenly, a big screen descended out of nowhere above our heads, and a live video started playing. Apart from the groom, everyone else turned around to see what was being played—it was a close-up of the bride entering the banquet hall. The cameraman kept his focus on the feet and moved the camera up—painfully slowly. It was easy to identify the bride. The quality of the video was not the best, but the bride had to be dressed in red and was walking in the middle of the crowd of other females. To her left was someone dressed in golden attire, and to her right was someone in pink—very bright pink.

The cameraman moved from their feet to the base of the varmala in Tamanna's hand. Purple and pink carnations, in an identical garland, were handed to Piyush for the ceremony by the bride's brother. I heard people tease Piyush as the bride came closer to the entry to the hall. It was all going well until I noticed the hand movements of the girl in gold. When you love someone and have been close to them for some time, you tend to recognize them from the simplest of things. The way her hands moved, the shape of her arms, the way she was walking—I instantly knew it was her! Suddenly, memories of Melbourne and before that flashed in front of my eyes, I felt a my blood gush to my head, and I was warm all over. Finally, the cameraman did us the immense favour of moving his lenses to the pretty faces, and I had eyes for only one among the crowd. She smiled as she accompanied her best friend. *She has lost so much weight; she has not been taking care of herself*, I felt small when I realized this. I had been so engrossed in pitying myself for the last months that I had forgotten to even consider whether she had a genuine problem, and that was why she had left all of a sudden.

The varmala ceremony ended, and I creepily kept on staring at Adira's face all the time—she did give me a brief look and a shy smile, but she was happily enjoying her best friend's wedding while I grinned like a monkey on drugs. How do I know how I looked? Well, I have evidence. I was standing closest to the groom as Adira was standing closest to the bride, and the cameraman captured my acts in candid close-up shots. If you are thinking of meeting the girl you love at a wedding and live in Delhi, check who the photographers are. If you hear the name Hunny and Bunny Lenses, and you are sure that it is Hunny who will cover the event, then take my advice—abort the mission, my friend. Do not attend the wedding if you do not want to be the butt of all jokes for months to come.

After the varmala I tried to talk to Adira a few times, but it is challenging to speak to a girl at her friend's wedding. Adira was always surrounded by other girls or guys till the time her friend was on the stage getting pictures clicked. There was not even a moment when our eyes met and she was free to talk to me. After the photo session was over, she became Tamanna's wing woman and climbed on the stage to help the bride manage her excessively burdensome attire. *Why do girls wear such heavy dresses that they need an army to help them walk even ten steps at their wedding!* Not that it makes any difference to me, nor do I care, especially if they are happy doing so. But on that occasion, I was being directly impacted by the weight of her dress and was not pleased about the situation.

The girls vanished into the den they had emerged from an hour ago to bedazzle us all, and I was left sulking in a corner. Adira was nowhere to be seen throughout the dinner and afterwards too. I had a quiet dinner with my dad while Mummy and other aunties in the family laughed and gossiped, hopping all over the venue. Finally, the guests started dispersing. The incredible thing about a north Indian Hindu wedding is the fact that people do not stay and witness the real wedding—the *phere,* the circumambulation around the sacred fire. The phere is usually after midnight, and only the close family stays back at the venue to see the couple getting married. The rest all disperse after enjoying the dinner.

This wedding was no different. After dinner the party thinned, and finally it was time for the mantras. The bride came back to the main hall where all the people, including Piyush, were eagerly waiting for her. Adira was family to her and could not leave her side. Later, as the pandit started chanting mantras, I spotted her standing alone, leaning against a wall in a quiet corner. Mummy and Dad sat sleepily at a table like most others. There was no one around to disturb us, so I approached Adira.

'Hi,' I whispered from behind her. I did not want to scare her, but my unintentional creepy act startled her a bit.

'Ohh! You scared me,' she said, with her eyes wide. I saw her forehead furrow, but she looked relieved, even happy, to see me.

'I am sorry. I did not mean to,' I was apologetic. It felt awkward, but we had to begin a conversation somehow.

'No, don't be. In fact, I am sorry,' she answered, taking me by surprise. I was not expecting her to apologize, I just wanted to know if she was okay, and why she was so thin and pale.

'I am sorry that I vanished like that after . . .' she continued.

Seeing her after so long was like a soothing balm on my bruised feelings, and as she stood fidgeting with her tiny handbag, looking for words, my concern for her grew greater. Her hands, which were always so small, had lost a considerable amount of flesh. Her eyes were the same, lively and gorgeous, but her face had shrunk and all I could see were her eyes and the dark circles under them.

'Are you okay?' I asked her after the pause became unbearable.

'Yes, I am fine,' she lied, looking straight into my eyes. Anyone, even people who did not know her, could have immediately guessed that there was something wrong with her, and I silently prayed that it was not to do with her physical health.

'But . . . but you look so pale and . . . weak,' I said, concerned, and she looked back at me like a child who has been told that they were caught eating mud in the backyard.

'My health is okay,' she said, and looked away from me in a failed attempt to hide her tears.

'I can see you crying. Tell me what happened,' I said soothingly, even though I was getting impatient with all the beating around the bush. Sometimes words do not have the power to shake someone up as much as a tiny teardrop. Her eyes had gone red, and I could no longer resist the urge to hold her hand and pacify her, and tell her that all would be fine. Though I did not know what was bothering her, I was reminded of what my mother often said to me—there is nothing in the world that is stronger than positive thoughts and determination.

'My parents have separated. They told me that they never loved each other, and that it was all a big mistake . . . a mistake . . . that they dragged with them for so many years . . . for my sake . . . Maybe, even I was a mistake . . .' she said, sobbing and leaning softly against my chest.

For many more minutes, she cried like a baby as she leaned against me, using me as her rock. Later, she told me that all this time she had been with her mother who was quite devastated after the separation; despite being aware that it was inevitable for the past many years. Adira never cried in front of her mother or any of her friends. She had not talked about the consequences that her parents' divorce had bought for her, not even with her best friend, Tamanna, as she was busy with her wedding, and Adira did not want to spoil her best friend's mood on her much-awaited wedding day.

'I am sorry about my behaviour after we came back to India,' she told me after a while. Her tears had dried up, and she was unwilling to talk about her parents any more, but she insisted on talking about 'us' and clearing the air.

I felt so tiny in front of her that I wanted to bury myself in the ground. There she was dealing with such a big crisis in her life and standing by her mother and giving her strength, while I was busy putting the blame on her. She had grown weak and pale in her attempt to put on a brave face, and I stood in front of her, trying to hide the 3-kg paunch that indulging in junk food and drinking beer had given me since she had gone away from me.

'You need not apologize to me. I have been in a much better state than you in the past months. In fact, I should be apologizing for going missing from your life when you needed me. For not being around when you were going through such a tough time in your life; for not being there when you needed a shoulder to cry on. I should have tried to find you and be with you when you needed a friend,' I told her. 'I should have been in touch regardless of what Angad said or meant that evening.'

'What did he say? When?' she asked me, raising her head. I narrated the whole incident that happened in Melbourne to her, and it turned out that she had never discussed anything with Angad or anyone else. 'Why would I? You know that I am a private person.' She was right. I knew that and should have called Angad's bluff, but instead of trusting her, I believed him and played into his hands. Also, she never gave her phone to him to answer my call on her behalf. She was not sure how he managed to answer—just some bad timing on my part, I guess. Maybe I called when she was not around, and Angad exploited the opportunity in his best interests.

'You are more than a friend to me, Raunak,' she took me by surprise and held both my hands. We looked at each other and magic happened. I remember the moment as if it happened this morning. She stood so close to me with a weak but genuine smile on her face and tilted her head just a little. It was the moment when we were supposed to kiss—this is how it happens in all the movies and fairy tales, doesn't it? But this was not a fairy tale or a movie; this was my life, so just when it was the perfect moment for us, I heard a loud female voice.

'Adira!' someone called her from behind.

'You didn't call me after that evening. I am still waiting for the call,' she told me, and turned away to join her friends. I stood there like a fool trying to comprehend what had just happened and if it was all for real and not a dream.

Sometime later, as the bride and groom took their last *phera* around the sacred fire and the ceremony was about to end, I took out my mobile and dialled her number.

'Adira! Happy Valentine's Day,' I said as soon as she answered.

'Happy Valentine's Day to you too,' she replied, and later that year she became my valentine.

Deciding to tell the story is the natural part; the decision takes no more than a few days of contemplation. A few days of your mind telling you the reasons why you should do it, on loop, is all it takes for you to pick up a notepad and a pen and write down all that is in your heart. The tough part is finding the right words to tell your story. And being neutral, unbiased and focused while doing so.

As I sit at my desk thinking about all that happened in the next few months in my story with Adira, I am worried that I might end up making one of us the guilty party and the other one the wronged one. Most likely, I will be biased towards myself, and unknowingly my words might make you see Adira as a person she is not. With the power of pen and paper, and the determination to narrate the story to the end, I have the responsibility of letting you decide.

As a writer, I do not have the liberty to influence the decision; instead, I present the facts and details. Do me a favour as you read it: keep an open mind, do not judge her or me. We were young, and unaware of the games destiny was capable of playing.

I am trying very hard to concentrate and find the right words to begin writing about this phase of our lives. The room that I am sitting in to write is quiet and dark; my own shadow is my sole companion here. While I sit here, looking blankly at my bright laptop screen, the screen saver comes up, it is a picture of us—when we had first started dating. The only sound that I can hear is my alarm clock ticking. I look at it to check what time it is—3.30 a.m. In the dark shadows that form on the walls, I can see outlines where once her pictures hung in delicate golden frames. 'Why golden?' I'd asked her the day she told me that it was her favourite colour. 'I love the colour. It is so magical. Just like the magical times that I spend with you.'

It is time to go to bed and close my eyes, for I have to go and meet someone extraordinary the next day. I shall tell you about this meeting at the end of the book.

For now, I consider the pop-up on the screen a sign from God and make a decision to recall everything I can from our first few days together after reuniting at Piyush's wedding.

14 FEBRUARY 2018

Usually, the first date gives you butterflies in your stomach, and you are prepared to impress. It is the first of many days to follow, after all, or at least you hope so. Honestly, I feel that first dates are over-hyped. In fact, every 'first' related to love and relationships is over-hyped, from the first date, first kiss, first hug, first touch, the first blah blah blah.

The fact is that everything becomes better with time when you are in love. If your first day with your girlfriend is the most memorable one, it means that you could never really develop the spark you had into a fire. Love is like wine—the older it gets, the better it becomes. It can intoxicate you, make you forget all your worries, and be the relief that you have always been looking for. The passion should increase day by day, hour by hour and minute by minute. People who say that the spark dies after the first few years have never been in love.

So, coming back to my first official date with Adira. It was a perfect day to go out with her—Valentine's Day—but the weather was definitely not ideal that morning. The sun never came out of the clouds, and the wind never stopped blowing on that cold, chilly day in February when all one could see, hear and feel was love. The harsh weather did not have the power to derail my plans of meeting Adira outside her hotel. The night before, I had asked her if we could go out the next day as she was staying in the city for one more day after the wedding. I was scared that she would say no, but like most things that we are usually scared of, this one too was just in my mind. She happily obliged and I was on top of the world. My first date with her—what else could I ask for? I could have asked someone to plan it for me, but I was not thinking of that at the time. Now, when I recall it, I think that a little planning would have hurt no one.

I had never been out on the streets or inside a mall on Valentine's Day in the past. What was the point of lurking and ogling at love-struck couples who had eyes for no one else, at least for that day? So, till the time we attended college, Piyush, Rohit and I spent the day at Nani's house. There was no point in attending the college either and witnessing all the red roses being passed around. That was the first year when all three of us had dates, and thus I had no one to talk to or to discuss what I should do and how I should approach the day.

When I called Adira on her mobile at 7 a.m. (talk about desperation), she was still in her bed and replied in monosyllables in a sleepy voice. She agreed to meet me outside her hotel at 12 p.m., and from there, I would take her to a mall. I thought it was the easiest and most practical plan.

Completely aware of the tricks luck was capable of playing on me, I sent her a text as well—just in case she forgot the time, or worse, she was sleep talking.

See you at 12 p.m. We are going to Great India Place, Noida.

Can't wait, came her reply, and our Valentine's Day date was officially on.

She is awake, I finally got busy looking for places to take her. Ten minutes later I had decided that we were going for a movie and then lunch. *You need to gift her something,* I reminded myself. As we were heading to a shopping mall, I could buy something for her on the spot. I was terrible at choosing gifts, so that made sense then!

Dressed in my favourite black UCB jacket and jeans, I was ready early. I hopped down the stairs to meet my first disappointment of the day; my ride was covered in dust. I had a beautiful, black, mighty bullet back then. I loved it more than my life, and at one point more than Adira too. It is hard to explain the kind of possessiveness I had for it—but I had had it for too long, and I was always very proud of my bike, and I loved it.

So, I picked up my bike, cleaned it to the best of my abilities, and reached her hotel in South Delhi half an hour early. I rang her number, hoping that she too was over-excited about the date and would be ready, but she wasn't. So, after killing half an hour here and there, I finally got to see her. I distinctly remember everything about our meeting that day. At 12 p.m. sharp, Adira came down to hypnotize me. Dressed in a light-pink salwar suit, she looked like a painting, and I was smitten by her as I saw her walk up to me in slow motion (I am not exaggerating). I could see her every movement in detail. Her walk from the exit door of the hotel to the other side of the road where I stood, dumbstruck, is still embossed on my mind. I think that moment was the highlight of the day for me, as things went downhill after that. I should have expected my day to take a nosedive after such a sparkly start as things are never that good—in movies maybe, but never in real life.

'Hi, where are we headed?' she asked the fool who was looking at her with his mouth open as he built pop-up air castles in his head at lightning speed.

'Noida.' I regained control of my open mouth, and suggested after an abrupt pause, 'Ammm . . . Great India Place?'

'Great!' she exclaimed, like a child who had just been promised a candy. I had to meet her expectations, and suddenly I felt a hefty weight on my shoulders, I had planned nothing, and she was looking forward to the day. I was less than impressed with myself, let down maybe.

Adira kept her delicate hands on my shoulders as she adjusted herself on the back seat, and became the first girl, who was not my relative, to sit on the back of my bike. Much to any guy's disappointment, she carefully placed her handbag between us and held on to the back support of the bike to keep herself steady as we rode. My dreams of being held by my waist went down the drain (damn all Hindi movies, for planting such expectations in the hearts of innocent young men)! I looked at her reflection in the rear-view mirror and smiled. Finally, we were on our way.

I had been to this mall a few times with my family and friends. It was usually a little more than overcrowded on weekends, but weekdays were quiet and relaxed. It was a Tuesday, and I had expected it to be more or less deserted. Much to my surprise, the mall was flooded with people in love. As far as my eyes could see, I saw the colour red and nothing else: red balloons, decorative banners, sale announcements, lights. Blood-red colour was everywhere, so much so that it was nauseating to look around. I love the idea of love, but who decided upon the colour of love? And why this overdose? I think love has no specific colours. It changes colours, as per the need, as per the relationship, as per the stage in your relationship, etc. Back then, I believed in the concept of Valentine's Day too. Now, I don't. After all, why is there a need for a particular day of love when every day should be special?

Anyhow, thanks to the raid by love-infected humans, none of my plans worked out. There were no tickets available that day, because all the other people who wanted to watch movies had booked in advance, unlike me. No decent restaurant would let us in as they had bookings. The tables which were not reserved had a wait time of at least one hour. With a rumbling tummy, I couldn't even think of what to do next. To add to my misery, people had been stomping on my feet every few minutes, as if they were punishing me for the date blunder.

Thankfully, Adira was not upset over the entire goof-up. 'Let us get some burgers, shall we?' she suggested, looking at me with bright eyes which had not lost their spark even after all the disappointment which had come our way.

'Sure,' I could not help but agree.

McDonald's was our saviour that day. In all the hustle and bustle, my plans of having a quiet conversation with her, holding her hands and maybe even hugging her, turned to ashes in front of my eyes. And just like that, it was time to head back. Time flew in her company or more to the point, in looking for a place to enjoy her company. Adira was staying with her mother who had come down for some legal work. She was waiting for her daughter to return so that they could head back to Chandigarh.

'When will you be back?' I asked her on our way out, hoping she would say 'soon.'

'Let us see,' she disappointed me with her answer as we headed towards the parking space.

So, nothing significant happened on our first date apart from her telling me that she had no immediate plans to come back to Delhi. However, that day was important for two reasons. Just as we got out of the elevator and stepped into the parking, she took out her phone. 'Let us take a picture to remember the day,' she said.

Her phone camera turned on, and our dark, blurry images froze in time. It was not the brightest or the best picture as the place had hardly any natural or unnatural light, yet it is one of my favourites till date, and it has been the screen saver on my laptop ever since. And some firsts are indeed special, like our first picture.

After we zoomed out of the parking, I remembered that I had forgotten to buy her a present. I apologized to her as many times as I could, all the way back, since it was too late to turn around and get something for her. When I had finally stopped apologizing for being so unprepared and forgetful, I tried to convince her to come back to Delhi. 'It will be great for us,' I recall telling her, and seeing her smile in the mirror.

Forty-five minutes later, we were outside her hotel. 'Bye. I like you a lot, and I'll think about it,' she said. Standing next to me and taking me by surprise, she gave me a gentle peck on my cheek—our first kiss. I know, it was just a peck, but it was worth a mention. It was cute, and it made me lose control of my bike a few times that evening as I replayed it in my head. It was magical. No violins played in the background; time didn't stop, I felt no sparks of electric current, but it did make my heart warm and told me that we were more than friends, finally.

By the time I came back home. Adira had sent me the picture she clicked of the two of us in the parking. The to and fro of messages lasted all night. At 2.13 a.m., I told her that I loved her, and at 3 a.m. she confirmed that she too had some feelings for me and wanted to get to know me before these feelings could be given a name. Sometime around 4 a.m. when she stopped messaging, I knew she had fallen asleep, and it was time for me to doze off as well, as the absences which I had taken for Piyush's wedding had come to an end, and I had to be at work in another five hours. But before I hit the sack, I had much more important work to finish. I spent the next half an hour going through our chat that night and grinning foolishly.

Maybe she was also in love with me.

LOOKING BACK IN TIME

Our lives were the happiest they could have been for the next three weeks. We were both always in touch over phones, emails, chats, and yet we could not get enough of each other, virtually. She was still in Chandigarh, contemplating whether getting a job near me was a good option for her mother. She was trying too hard to be a good daughter, and it made me fall for her all the more crazily.

So, while my work life sucked and I was the one who was blamed for all the pending work at the office, I was content and looked forward to each sunrise; to getting into the metro and calling her to hear all about what she had to tell me that day. I also realized that I was a great listener, for most of our conversations were her sweet chitter-chatter and my dull verbal nods and laughter. I was so embarrassed to not be contributing enough to the discussions that I asked her more than a few times if she was getting bored talking to me, more than once a day at least. I think at that point all she needed was a listening ear, some empathy, and assurance that all will be fine soon and she need not pressurize herself so much. 'You are doing great,' was all she longed to hear from people, but people seldom show empathy.

Her mother had her own demons to fight and didn't notice that her child suffered silently beside her. Days were filled with lovely messages, long phone calls and midnight chats for the two of us. Finally, my work was not the most critical part of my life.

Before being in the nameless relationship that Adira and I had, I always wondered what people in love talked about, and how they managed to have so many conversations, one after the other, all day, every day with each other. It is quite evident that after a certain point they would run out of topics to talk about, wouldn't they?

If you wonder the same, then all I can tell you is to wait. Just wait until you are smitten by someone. Wait until you are bitten by the love bug. It crawls into your head and creates a space that you never knew existed. All of a sudden, your brain thinks of the things you want to know about her: small things, more substantial items, things that matter to her and also the ones that don't. You want to know everything. Like I never knew she loved morning walks. I never woke up early enough to catch her going out for a walk early in the morning and coming back to the house without anyone knowing while she stayed with Nani. None of my friends knew that either, I am sure of it.

I did not know how much she loved soft, romantic music, especially old Bollywood numbers—exactly like me. But unlike me, she had quite a melodious voice and hummed along beautifully. I was banned from singing at home, or a warning was issued by my parents in the public interest. She, however, sang whenever she was happy, or when she knew that I was upset over something. She sang when she was on a call with me, and also when she cooked. She loved cooking food, especially when she was stressed.

How well did she know how to cook? It was for me to know in the next few months. When I initially detested Samba and was too scared to even touch him but slowly had become quite fond of my pug buddy, she told me that she had a pet dog when she was a child. That dog was her first friend, but her mother hated dogs because of all the mess they made. 'I want to get a dog as soon as I move out alone,' she told me casually at the end of that conversation, and I knew I had to get one for her.

We were so alike in many ways and yet so different in others. I had studied in the same school with the same set of friends all my life, while she changed schools eight times before she finally settled in the one where she befriended Tamanna.

So, the topics just kept sprouting from nowhere, but there were also a few times when both of us ran out of things to talk about. Killing the silence with a question, 'So, what else?' that lingered in the air for a while until one of us revisited one of our previous conversations and we laughed over it. Sometimes, just hearing her voice was enough to keep the conversation going, and the sound of her laughter was like heroin for me; I was under her spell.

In fact, both of us were in the phase where it is all so good that you pinch yourself a few times a day to see if it is real and not a dream. All was golden around us, and for those weeks, and many more weeks that followed, we only needed each other. I had been pressing her to come back, and she had started giving a few interviews. She was worried about her mother being alone but knew that both of them had to move on.

Finally, one Monday, she called me early in the morning. It was a set pattern for us—texts in the morning while I was at home, and then I used to call her when I boarded the metro. I was sitting with my parents, enjoying my morning tea when her number flashed on my phone screen. I excused myself and answered her call in the balcony. 'Hi. Good morning,' I said, not hiding my surprise.

'I got the job,' she told me chirpily, giggling like a child. Placements for an IT giant were happening at a place near her mother's house in Chandigarh. They were hiring communication experts for their company. Adira had been an English language student at college, which made it easier for her to get the job.

'Awesome!' I exclaimed, and found my mother standing behind me. She had followed me like a cat to the balcony. Avoiding her eyes, I told Adira I would call her back as soon as I could. She was going to be upset with me for not talking more, and I knew it. But handling her mood, which by then I knew how to change in ten minutes, was more doable than managing the hundreds of questions my mother would have asked me had she sniffed anything like love in the balcony.

Nani already had a PG that year which meant that Adira was to live somewhere else. She had to come to Delhi a week later, and we started looking for a house for her. Three days was all it took to finalize a home in Noida, near her new office—a flat her mother had suggested she stay in.

18 MARCH 2018

Early that morning, I picked up Adira from the New Delhi metro station in my father's car, and we headed to her new home in Noida. I was seeing her after so many days which had changed the texture of our relationship and brought new feelings for us. I was nervous as well as anxious before the meeting, but seeing her took all my nervousness away and filled me with anticipation and hope.

We stuffed the boot of the black Swift with her numerous bags and began our journey. The weather was starting to warm up, and with the windowpanes down, warm wind blew on our faces. Memories of the little time that we spent together at Piyush's wedding surfaced in my head and soon found their way into our conversation. The one-hour drive came to a halt at Sector 60, Noida. Adira's mother had found her an apartment in a beautiful high-rise building. The house belonged to her mother's friend who lived in Mumbai and needed someone to live there so that it was not misused by the notorious goons around.

'Are you sure you want to stay alone here?' I asked her again, and frustration replaced her happy smile.

'Why do you keep on asking this question all the time?' she replied a bit angrily. 'Tenth floor,' she added as we stepped into the unmanned lift.

'Because, had it been a safe place your mother's friend would not have been so concerned about it being unoccupied,' I told her for the umpteenth time, and saw a faint smile appear at the corners of her lips.

'I am not a child. Moreover, I now want to live as an adult, alone; not in some PG where there are people to feed you and tell you when to come and when to go out of the house,' she said, as if I were the one who could not see the obvious.

'Also, I don't think boys can stay over at PGs,' she said as she tilted her head and gave me a knowing smile. *Is she talking about me? Or someone else? Does she want me to stay over with her?*

Things were happening a little too fast, not that I was complaining. Had they happened at the pace I wanted them to, we would be fifty before our first kiss!

We were greeted by an elderly couple as we got out at the tenth floor who looked at us shamelessly from top to toe to form their opinions about us; without even being aware of our first names. That is what the world is like nowadays—judging everyone and anyone you meet, see or hear about. No one knows anything about the people around them, yet we all have our opinions.

'Hold on,' Adira instructed me, and started looking for the keys to the apartment in her handbag. It was a large tote—I know that now; she made me aware of a few different kinds of handbags. Totes were her favourite as she could carry all that she needed and also stuff all that she might need once in her life into the bag. It took her nearly ten minutes to fish out the keys which were on a large keychain with a yellow, smiling minion attached to it.

'You took so much time to take this out?' I said jokingly, and from that moment on, the day nose-dived like an airplane which had lost both its wings and the pilot had been knocked unconscious. She did not appreciate my joke.

We entered the well-lit place, and I put her bags in the living area. The apartment was well-furnished. It had three bedrooms, one living area and a well-maintained kitchen. I took a stroll through the house and complimented the place. Adira refused to acknowledge any of my attempts to soothe her hurt ego. I was not at fault as she did take way too long to find the keys that were attached to an object nearly as big as a rabbit. Yet, I made as many efforts as I could to lighten her mood. She started responding in monosyllables after a while. That gave me a little confidence, and I decided to bridge the physical gap between us.

Desperate? Who, me? No, I was way beyond desperate!

I started brushing her hands with mine and softly touching her arms at every opportunity as we cleaned the house and made it liveable.

It took us a little more than a couple of hours to brush off the small cobwebs and dust the furniture. 'What about lunch?' she asked, crashing on the sofa after everything was done.

'We can go out for lunch, and we can get some kitchen essentials on our way back,' I suggested.

'Great,' she replied, and got up to face me. The same fluttering feeling which I had experienced the first time I had seen her invaded my senses.

I looked at her; she was so close to me, and her face somehow looked softer. Her expression was warm, and so were my ears with the flow of blood into my head. I took the liberty to hold her hand and squeeze it. She gave me a smile, and I knew that it was the moment for us—the moment when we were supposed to kiss; to say the least.

My stupid phone gave out a loud, shrill scream, which shattered my dreams into many pieces. 'I am sorry,' I said, struggling to take it out of my pocket. 'It is my mother,' I looked at her apologetically, and she took a step back.

'It's okay,' I could see her injured expression.

'Hello,' I answered the call and walked towards her balcony where the sun shone, leaving her in the room and expecting her to be waiting for me. When I returned after the call, she was still there but the moment had passed.

'There is a good Chinese place nearby,' she told me, looking up from her phone and smiling.

'Let's eat,' I agreed with her, and abruptly looked away, hoping that she didn't see in my eyes the thoughts that had been running in my head earlier, while secretly also hoping that she did.

I picked up my car keys, and she picked up her tote before we locked the house and made our way to the elevator.

'It was my mother. My sister has not been keeping very well, and my mother might have to go to be with her, in London,' I tried to explain the reason for the phone call, and she told me that she understood.

'Thank you for all your help today,' she said simply, as the elevator descended to the ground floor. She took a step in my direction and stood facing me, as close as the space permitted us to be to each other. This time no phone calls came our way, and we had our first kiss, in the moving elevator, with security cameras on us. Sometimes, the place does not matter, even when it should.

We came out of the lift like culprits and giggled as we reached our car, where I told her that I loved her, and for the first time, I heard her say those three magical words to me, 'You are silly!'

She said this whenever I told her that I loved her.

It was her version of I love you too.

30 MARCH 2018

Despite almost being in the same city, Adira and I could not meet again after the day she arrived. She had joined her office almost immediately and had found new friends. I knew that she was not very happy with my absence because I was the one who had convinced her to leave her mother alone in Chandigarh. Having convinced her to leave her family, I became busy with mine, leaving her alone. Honestly, things at home were beyond my control, and no matter how much I wanted to see her again and be in her company, I could not.

The day after Adira came to Delhi, my mother got a worrying phone call from my sister who was in London and expecting a baby. She was bedridden, unable to do most of her work on her own as she had a complicated pregnancy, and had no one to help her there. After many days of contemplation and numerous consultations with almost all our relatives, my parents decided to go to the UK and support her as that was the need of the hour. Dad took a sabbatical from work and Mummy got on with preparations.

My next two weekends were spent sorting out their travel documents and shopping with my parents—for them, for my sister and for the tiny baby who was yet to arrive on the planet. Adira and I managed to be in touch with each other over the phone. We had long conversations about our days each morning and evening as our office timings were similar, but I felt bad that I could not give her the time she deserved. I knew that I had to give her more of my time, and felt like a culprit every time she suggested a meeting, and I gave an excuse for why it was not feasible to meet her.

Finally, on Thursday 30 March, my parents took an early morning flight to London. My mother was in tears as she was concerned about my well-being once I was alone. I assured her that I was a grown-up and could look after myself. In fact, at that time I really wanted them to go so I could be alone for some days; I wanted to be an adult. 'Relax, Mummy,' I hugged her at the point beyond which they were to travel alone.

'Eat on time, and do not overwork,' she said as she hugged me tight, wiping away her tears. And a couple of minutes later, off they went.

The first thing that I did once they were out of sight was to text my sister informing her of their departure. She would see it when she woke up in London. As soon as I was out of the airport, the reality sank in—for the first time in my life, I was going to live alone in my own house for the next six months. To be honest, the thought was not very comforting. It was 7.30 a.m., the time when Adira had usually boarded her morning metro to her office. I called her but she didn't pick up, which disappointed me a little. Later I got a text saying that she was busy and would call back in a while.

That day, as I was so close to work already, I decided to take the car and ditch the metro for a change. I planned to catch up with Adira after work, and then drop her back home for an unplanned dinner date. As I drove to work that morning, I kept an eye on my phone, hoping for a call or text from her. I reached work and rechecked my phone. Nothing. This concerned me, and I decided to make a call to see if all was okay at her end.

I dialled her number, and she answered the call after a few rings. She sounded chirpy and her usual happy self. Phew! I was worried that she was furious with me as I had cancelled a meeting with her just last night. It was a party invite with her office colleagues, and as I knew no one apart from her, I had skipped it. I had thought she might not even answer my calls. I told her about my plans for the two of us that evening—a dinner date after work. 'I can pick you up from your office,' I suggested. I was really excited about finally spending some time alone with her without having to worry about pending work back home, but she poured ice-cold water on my excitement with her response.

She declined with a simple 'I can't today, I am sorry. I have made some plans already.'

Is she punishing me?

'Oh, okay,' I could manage nothing more as I was not expecting the conversation to go in that direction. *Way too confident of yourself all the time*, my own mind was making fun of the soup I was in. I wondered what she had planned. I always struggled to find the words to ask her in a way that didn't annoy her with my interference in her life, or make her feel that I was one of those men who could not see their girl hang out with men, which I was, to be honest.

There is soft music playing in the background. She is definitely not taking the metro to work today. She is in a car. Yes, I can hear some honking. She is definitely in a car, or maybe a cab as she didn't have a car of her own. She is probably in a friend's car; perhaps that friend is giving her a lift in her car, or his. A male friend, a man—shut up! My mind was wandering off again.

Thankfully, I didn't have to ask her any questions. She went on to explain on her own, after an awfully long silence while my brain was still working on the question.

'I am with an old friend from school,' she told me, as if she could read my mind, which was borderline creepy, to say the least. 'We have planned to catch up after work for a movie and dinner tonight. As you and I had no plans, I promised,' her innocent voice made me feel so petty, but only for a moment. She never mentioned her friend's gender. And she never even once said that she would cancel her plans for me when she should have offered. Not that I would have stopped her from going. Or maybe I would have, but she did not know that. *She should have provided at least told me the name of this 'old friend from school'* . . .

'Give her some space; she will have male friends who are not her boyfriends. Not all men are in love with the same girl you love,' this is the advice I would have given my younger self. I know better now. You might be thinking this, but it is easier said than done—especially when the girl in question is so pretty. I could feel my nerves panicking, and my heart was pounding.

'Ya, I know, I wanted to surprise you,' I tried to add some romance to my impromptu plan, hoping she would cancel her other appointment and join me for dinner instead. But I also knew that I was wrong in hoping to persuade her to cancel her plans so I quickly added, 'I can pick you up from the party and drop you home. Like that, we will get to meet at least.' I felt my voice almost cracking up, sounding feeble at the end, to say the least.

I knew very well that she had patiently waited for me to fulfil my personal commitments, and now was my time to trust her. But insecurity doesn't listen to all the valid points in an argument; it doesn't bother to analyse the situation. It just throws the door open, walks in and conquers your thoughts—just the way it happened that morning with me.

'I will manage, don't worry. I shall call you tonight,' she said a little too dryly, and I had no other reason to prolong our conversation. We bid flat goodbyes and got on with our day.

I am sure she had a blast that day; mine too was quite eventful. I had thoughts of Adira, with men swooning all over her, exploding inside my skull. I spent my day amidst innumerable creepy, weird ideas that zoomed in and out of my head. Little did I know that when I thought that it was the world against my love, it was me who was against it. I was standing in my own way and was blinded by jealousy which had no reason to exist whatsoever.

After an uneasy day, walking into an empty house added to my miseries. I called my parents on my return from work. They had reached London safely and were gaga about the place. They had even made plans to settle there permanently, that too within one hour of their plane landing at the airport. That was the moment I figured out where my 'air-castle-building genes' came from. But their happy voices were the only good things that happened to me that evening. I enjoyed talking to them about their small adventure at the expense of my sister and brother-in-law. After a one-hour-long call, we bid our goodbyes, and I had my cold food that the tiffin wallah had dropped outside my door before I came back from work. Mummy had arranged for my food to be delivered two times a day via a tiffin service for the time she was not around. After having their meal that evening, I was not sure if I intended to keep the arrangement going. But that was a small issue—the main problem was that I was still waiting to hear from Adira. She did not call me back that evening, and demons were at work again with flashes of her with other men invading my dreams. I was in and out of sleep all night, checking my phone for a message or a phone call from her. Finally, at 2 a.m. when I hadn't slept at all, I messaged her on WhatsApp:

Goodnight, I was waiting for your call.

It was delivered. A moment later two ticks appeared, but they did not turn blue. Waiting for her to read and respond to my text, I do not know when sleep took over my senses at last.

31 MARCH 2018

It was a Friday, and I was working from home on Fridays that month. I had forgotten to set the alarm on my phone as well as the alarm clock, which was the only object that had stayed in the same place on my bedside table for years. Waiting for Adira's call last night, and tossing in the bed for hours, ensured that my eyes opened way past the usual time.

Thanks to our *kaam-wali bai* (maid), I was finally awake at 11 a.m. 'Shit!' I exclaimed as soon as I checked the wall clock in the drawing room. Our maid (Shanti) had been with us since I could remember. She was roughly my age; married with four kids, or maybe more. I knew about four of them. She used to come to our home to do the household chores with her mother when I was a kid. I never gave it a thought then, but now I realize how difficult her life must have been. While we cribbed and fought for toys and games which we believed were our birthrights in our childhood, she never had a real childhood. She was married off at an early age to a construction worker, and from what I knew from Mummy, she was now the sole breadwinner of her house. Although she was the maid, she had a set of our house keys with her, which she never bothered to bring along. Mummy trusted her way more than she trusted her own son. Shanti rang the bell only once on days when I was alone at home and waited patiently for me to answer the door. Unlike the other days, she had already rung the bell three times as she told me.

'Bhaiya, are you not well? I had to ring the bell three times,' she asked me as soon as she stepped in, embarrassing me further.

'I overslept,' I told her honestly, and she got on with the household chores. Leaving her to it, I dashed back into my bedroom to check my phone. No messages or phone calls from her—my anger turned into concern, and I dialled her number fearing the worst.

'Hi, good morning,' she greeted me, answering the call quickly.

'Hi,' I was thankful that she sounded okay, and within seconds of knowing that, my anger returned. 'I was expecting a call from you last night after you got back home,' I could not help telling her that I was not pleased.

'I know, it just slipped my mind, and by the time I recalled that you must have been expecting my call, it was too late. It was 10 p.m. already,' she explained.

10 p.m.! 10 p.m. was late? I was tossing in my bed till 2 a.m.! Like a pancake on a hot, well-greased pan, and she thought that 10 p.m. was late? I gasped in astonishment and wanted to say something, but she had a lot to talk about. So, I decided not to spoil the conversation.

'I saw your message in the morning and thought you must have been sleeping. Acha, I wanted to tell you all about yesterday. We had so much fun. I also met some of my other schoolmates . . .' she sounded happy, and I did not want to spoil her mood by bringing up the topic of other men in her life. She was on her way to work on the metro, and I was roaming around the house in my pyjamas—who else in the world had time if we did not!

We had a long chat about her friends and their work, my work, my friends and my family for about one hour when she said, 'I think we should start talking a little about "us" as well,' and giggled. Yes, we should, and I wanted to see her so badly. It had been ages!

'Yes, and we should meet too,' I chipped in.

'I am sorry for cancelling our plans yesterday. Can we catch up today?'

Yes, yes—I was dying to hear these words all through your excited blabbering about your friends in the last many minutes.

'Shall I pick you up after work?' It was not too cold any more for a romantic bike ride to Connaught Place for a coffee date.

'Are you sure? You will have to drive all the way here and then go back,' she asked. It was indeed going to be a super-long drive to and fro for me. That was the moment when I realized that love is a little silly, apart from being all the other things that it is. We agreed to meet at 5 p.m. outside her office.

I was parked outside her office at 4.30 p.m. sharp. It was all so new for me. Not the love—I was in love with her for so long that it did not feel new at all; it was more like a part of who I was. Arriving on time or early was new for me. I was known to be the last person to arrive anywhere and everywhere. Sometimes this talent of mine reached new heights when I completely forgot that I was supposed to be somewhere; it happened rarely, but it did happen. Those were the occasions when I would get a phone call from a friend asking me where I was while I was in the shower or in bed, or worse still, asleep.

So, being on time and waiting for someone was an exciting feeling that day too. I parked my bike under the shade of a tree where I could see the exit door of her office. It was a windy day, and the sun had been out for only a few minutes. I wore my favourite black-and-red jacket, which acted as a shield against the wind. I was not sure if Adira was carrying a coat or a jacket with her that day, so I'd taken another jacket with me for her, just in case she needed it. Considerate? Me? No, I was not willing to part with my own clothes to keep her warm. I was more selfish than polite.

She stepped out of her office dressed in a pair of blue jeans and a white T-shirt. I had guessed right. As expected, there was no warm clothing in sight. She waved goodbye to her friends and walked towards me, beaming with happiness. Her tresses were all over her face, and she kept adjusting them as she crossed the road with the chilly wind blowing from every direction. She looked adorable.

'Hi, bike?' she asked me, concerned.

'Don't like it?' I asked her, knowing that she was worried about the cold weather.

'Isn't it a bit cold for a bike ride? Where are we going?'

I had not told her yet that I had planned a long ride.

'CP,' I told her, and grinned.

'I might die before we enter Delhi on this bike,' she managed to say with her teeth chattering.

I took her away her worries and magically offered her a thick grey jacket. 'For me?' she asked, taking it from my hand and wearing it.

My jacket was two sizes too big for her, and she looked as if her face were lost somewhere in the fur at the collar. She gave an impression of a child in their father's jacket, and I could not contain my laughter at the sight of her.

'What?' she asked, knowing why I was laughing and joining in. With the jacket on, Adira was all set to brace the cold weather, and I could not stop beaming at my forward planning. She hopped on the back of my bike, kept her hands on my shoulders, and off we went. This time, her bag remained on her shoulder.

With the cold breeze returning, the streets were more or less deserted. People prefer to stay in when the weather turns cold. There was hardly any traffic and fewer honking cars. We chatted all the way to the coffee shop. In no time, we had reached Barista in Connaught Place.

The place was quite the opposite of what we had experienced on the roads. It was filled with people, mainly couples in love, who needed a warm, cosy space and had somewhat less money in their pockets. All the tables were booked. People were queuing up at the counter to buy coffee. The ones that had managed to secure a table had empty cups and glasses resting on their tables but didn't make space for the new customers. No one wanted to leave the warm coffee shop and face the windy weather outside.

'We will not get a table here,' Adira declared, and I agreed with her, 'Let's check somewhere else,' she suggested.

We kept on hopping from one coffee shop to another, but the scene inside remained the same.

'Let's go to my house, I shall make some chai for both of us.' Her plan sounded more promising than any of the staff's suggestions. They had told us to linger for some time and wait for people to disperse and give up their comfortable seats for us. I understood their problem as well as those who were not willing to move out and face the chilly weather.

'Are you sure?' I looked at her tired face. Her small nose had turned a deep pink due to the cold wind. She had tucked her hands under her armpits for warmth. I too had lost all my energy in the cold weather. Even the flame in her eyes could not keep me warm enough to bear the cold without a hot beverage. I knew that Adira had slogged for eight hours already at work, and now all that ping-pong from one coffee shop to another had drained her even more. I didn't want to bother her more by forcing her to make chai at her home, but I did not want her to get more tired either. Apart from all that, my main worry was that I had never been alone with a girl, in her house, in my entire life. I was worried about my reaction, or rather the lack of it.

'Yes, I am sure,' she replied, rubbing the back of her neck. She was definitely exhausted, so I gave in. Honestly, I did not trust myself, and under no circumstances could I ask her to trust me either. I didn't want to do something stupid and hurt our relationship, which gave me all the more reason to be sceptical.

We reached her building and parked the bike in the guest parking zone. She led the way as we took the elevator and reached the tenth floor. She fished out her house keys, switched on the first two lights and welcomed me in with a hand gesture. 'Home sweet home,' she said smiling.

'I know, I have been here before,' I reminded her, tapping the forefinger of my right hand on my temple.

'Ya, I know, but I have made a few changes since the last time you were here,' she said, raising her eyebrows, and added, 'feel free to look around while I make two cups of chai for us.' The house was pleasantly warm, and I felt an instant rush of blood in my body once she closed the door behind us and busied herself in the kitchen.

I took a leisurely tour of her house and noticed that she had added some really tiny details to her home—a few candles, decorative plants, strings of LED lights, clocks, pots, pictures of her with her mother and other stuff that most guys hardly care about. She had transformed one of the bedrooms into a mandir and had lit up many lights in it. By the time I came back to the living area, she had turned the heating on and jackets were no longer necessary.

Then I strolled into the kitchen. 'You have a mandir now. It looks great.'

'Thanks, but there is a lot more than just the mandir that is new. For instance, this jar is new,' she told me, pointing towards a jar which was filled with assorted grains and sat on the kitchen island. I had not noticed it, and honestly did not understand what it was or why it was being mentioned.

'Okay,' I said, inspecting it to please her as she poured our chai into big coffee mugs.

'Do you want something to go with it?' she asked me, opening the top drawer for me to see what was available to eat and choose something. My crazy eyes, however, followed the hem of her T-shirt which lifted up and exposed a bit of her waist. She caught me in this shameful and lecherous act and quickly repositioned her arm.

'No, nothing,' I was too embarrassed to look in her direction.

Quietly, I followed her into the living area, and we sat with our tea in our hands, looking at the view outside from her high-rise building as we quietly sipped the chai. I do not remember much when it comes to the taste of our chai that evening, but I can tell you that Adira makes the worst chai anyone could possibly make. Even Rohit makes better chai than her. That evening, after all the tiredness and then after being caught ogling her waist, anything felt bearable, even 'that' chai. I do not recall giving her any wrong reviews on her chai-making skills that evening.

Five minutes of deadly silence later, Adira asked me about my family—my sister to be specific. I told her that both my parents and my sister were in good spirits, and a normal conversation about routine stuff followed.

'Were you angry with me yesterday? You sounded like you were,' she asked me, and I decided not to lie.

'I was, but then I realized that I cannot just bind you to me. You have a life, and we had made no plans to meet . . .' That was the moment when she took away the empty cup from my hand and our fingers brushed, making me forget all the words and sounds my mother had once taught me as a child.

After all the anxiety and anger that had built up in me last night, the sudden closeness and affection made me lose my mind. Thankfully, Adira had missed me too, as she told me later. She let me hold her hand and bring her closer to me to hug her. I felt her scent, The One by D&G. The same smell fill my senses and her warmth light up my spirit. I wanted to kiss her more than ever. I slid my hand around her waist and pulled her towards me. She put her arms around me, and soon she was running her fingers through my hair. I couldn't wait any longer and held her face as we looked into each other's eyes. The next moment we were passionately kissing each other, our eyes closed as we only felt each other. We were in a world of our own where nothing remained but the two us. I pulled her even closer and held her more tightly. She did the same as we continued to kiss. And then suddenly my phone rang. It was in my pocket, and the noise was unbearable.

We broke our embrace, and I struggled to pull the phone out and silence it. The call was from an unknown number, so I disconnected it without a second thought and held her again. However, the caller had decided to spoil our moments of togetherness, and the phone rang again. 'It is an unknown number,' I said, flashing the screen at her and hiding my frustration.

'Let me see,' Adira said quite unexpectedly.

'It is my mom,' she told me with her eyes wide open and rushed to check her phone. I disconnected the call. This time I was scared of answering it. Adira rushed back into the living room. Her face was pale. 'She has not called me. Why is she calling you? Where did she get your number from? She doesn't even know about you yet!'

'Are you sure it is your mother's phone number?' I asked her, and started reading it aloud, 'nine seven one seven . . .'

'. . . Eight one eight' she completed the number for me. 'Yes, I know it is her, but why is she calling you? And where did she get your number?' she repeated. I was worried too. *Why was she calling me? And how on earth did she get my number!*

'Call her back,' Adira commanded.

'And tell her what?' I asked in a loud voice.

'Tell her nothing, just ask her who she is and why has she been calling . . .' Before Adira could say anything more, the phone rang again.

'What if she is outside and she knows we are together?' I was worried about being caught with Adira when we were alone for the very first time, that too by her mother, even though I wasn't doing anything much with her daughter.

She sprang towards the door and peered outside to check just in case her mother was indeed out there, which she wasn't. Adira then called the security room to check if she had had another guest that evening, her mother. She was not there!

'Call her back and see what happens,' she told me one more time after she was quite sure that her mother was undoubtedly not nearby.

I did not want to look like a coward, so I called her mother back, half hoping that she was now too busy to answer my call. Luck is hardly ever in my favour, and her mother answered the call before the first ring could be completed.

'Hello,' she said in a calm voice. There was no anger, hatred or threat in her tone, yet I felt all three coming my way from her in an inexplicable way.

'Hello,' I muttered meekly, and waited for her to say something.

'Yes?' she surprised me with a question, hinting that she was not aware of the reason why I had called her. It puzzled me, and I looked at Adira for help. She looked at me, wondering what was going on. She could not hear her mother on the other end, but she knew that I was losing confidence with every passing minute.

'I am returning your call; there was a missed call,' she said.

'Actually . . . I got . . . I got a call from this number. Your number,' I replied as my heart pounded.

'Oh, okay. Ummm . . . Are you looking for a house to rent? I am a property agent,' she lied to me outright, and asked my name.

'Raunak,' I replied without a thought, and she abruptly hung up on me.

Later, we got to know that Adira's mobile bill had been delivered to her mother's house that day. It was a regular customized bill with details of her calls to me. Her mother wanted to protect her child from falling for a man who was not right for her, just as her mother had, years ago. This phone call was an attempt to figure out who had been talking to her daughter for hours every day, that too at her expense. Adira got a call from her mother a few moments after she hung up on me to inquire about 'Raunak' and the never-ending phone calls.

The least that I can say about my unpleasant phone conversation with the woman I hoped to call my mother-in-law one day is that the call was the beginning of a very strained relationship between the two of us. She hated me—still hates me. She did tolerate me for a while for the sake of her daughter, but only enough to let me be around her. For her, I was the man who was conspiring to take away her only daughter from her. She was not going to let that happen so easily.

Adira's mother warned her to stop seeing me, unaware that she was more than seeing me a few moments ago, in her own house. Thankfully, she was not around and didn't know anything about my daring act of entering her daughter's living room. After the phone call ended, neither of us could think or talk about anything other than her mother. I bid Adira goodbye half an hour later and headed back home, still shivering under my clothes.

THE BLISSFUL SUMMER

Even though both Adira and I were living alone in our own homes, we used to meet each other when we were out. Neither of us felt comfortable about breaking her mother's trust by going home, the way we'd done earlier.

My parents called me every evening to keep me company while I ate the cold tiffin food every evening. My sister was due to deliver any day, and they were both excited about becoming grandparents. They had made a few visits to the hospital already because of false alarms.

Adira and I spent every weekend together, shopping or relaxing in a shopping mall near her house. We took long bike rides to Delhi, India Gate mainly, and enjoyed late-night ice creams before I dropped her home after every date. More than a few times, I wanted to go in and be with her all night long, holding her in my arms and talking about our future, our present and laughing over the past. Yet every time I reached her building, I recalled her mother's tone on the phone that evening, and it killed my enthusiasm. I imagined her to be hiding somewhere, maybe behind the bushes, keeping an eye on her daughter, waiting for me to take a step towards her so that she could come out and pounce on me, with a deadly knife.

Otherwise, things were going great in our lives. Adira had adjusted well in her new job and made a few friends who approved of me. I was happy with my job and loved her more every passing day. We were so perfect for each other. We both loved food, reading, old Hindi songs, bike rides. It was all too good to be true, but it was real—the most beautiful reality of my life.

After three months into each other's company, so many calls, meetings, dates, kisses and hugs, we were yet to have our first fight. Not that I was waiting for it, but I knew that a fight was lurking around the corner. I even knew the reason why we would fight—her mother. We did have a few arguments about the kind of unnecessary hatred that she had for me without even knowing me, meeting me or seeing my picture. Every evening, her mother would call Adira to see if she had company. Every weekend when we were out for a date, her mother would want to talk to 'a girl' to ensure that she was not out alone with me. Around the same time, Piyush had dropped out of his MBA course in America and had returned to Delhi with Tamanna. They were looking for a house to settle in, and we begged Tamanna to provide an alibi for Adira every time Adira's mother called her. Adira would put them on a conference call just to make her feel that Tamanna and Piyush were always with us. Her mother trusted the couple more than she trusted her own daughter. Her trust in me was in negative figures. Sometimes, we even planned and went on double dates with Tamanna and Piyush as her mother wanted to explore the option of video calls.

I was more upset with Adira than with her mother as she would not even let me click any pictures together. She would say, 'Mummy has told me not to.' She would not change her status or hide her 'single' status on Facebook as she didn't want to irk her mother. I was infuriated, to say the least, and to add salt to my wounds was the fact that I was living alone and wanted her for myself sometimes—no shopping, no movies, just the two of us at my home, talking laughing, cooking maybe. I was sick of roaming around in the same malls every time. But I didn't have the guts to speak to her about it. She wanted to be with me. I knew it because she had invited me to her house almost every time I dropped her home, but I was so scared to go in there and too much of a chicken to ask her to stay with me for a few days.

21 JULY 2018

It was my birthday, and it was a Sunday too. For a change, I had to work all day on Saturday as well, because I was the only one who had not sent in my report which was to be discussed at work with the client on Monday. I had taken a few days off work from the coming Monday onwards as I wanted to catch up on my sleep and give some time to my family in the UK virtually, as my sister was all set to give birth.

I had been working from home on Friday as well. Adira had planned a shopping spree with her new work friends that day, and we had hardly contacted each other, apart from a phone call at the end of the day. We had last met on the weekend prior to my birthday as I had been busy with work all that week too. My mother called me at night on Saturday a few times to keep me updated on my status of becoming a brand-new uncle, and she was the first one to wish me a happy birthday.

After another false alarm a week ago, they were back at the hospital again—this time to be told that the baby was due any moment. It was my birthday the next day, and I was rooting for the baby to wait one more day, unconcerned about the pain my sister had to go through for so many hours, just so that the baby and I could share our birthdays. The good news is that we do share our birthdays.

I conveyed the news of my sister being in hospital to Adira that evening when we spoke over dinner, separately in our own homes. She was enjoying a cheese burst pizza from Domino's while I stuffed myself with a rather unappealing-looking portion of biryani, which for some reason tasted funny. At 12.12 a.m., she called me again to wish me a happy birthday.

When I woke up the next day, I felt a sudden urge to use the loo, even before my body was completely awake. It was unusual for my body to get into cleaning mode before I had bribed it with a few cups of tea. Not thinking much of it and ignoring the constant dull ache in my stomach, I went on with my day. I called Adira, had a few cups of tea, called Adira again to confirm the meeting place and time, had one more cup of tea, and went to the loo more than a dozen times before accepting that I was down with something, most likely stomach flu—*Damn! The biryani!*

It was too late do anything about it. By 11 a.m., I was sweating like a pig and was dehydrated—like a dog under the sun. *You have no other choice*, my mind and body did not need a lot of convincing to cancel the plans. *Adira will be disappointed, and it has been days since you guys have met*, was the last insane thought that dared to creep into my head before I felt my stomach growl for the umpteenth time and sent the text to her.

Sorry, baby. Unwell. Can't meet.

As expected, my phone started ringing within moments. It must be her. I knew that, but I was stuck in the bathroom while the phone rang continuously for minutes, call after call, in the living room. After a few tiring yet relieving minutes, I came out and checked my phone. There were twenty-three missed calls, sixteen WhatsApp texts and three messages on my phone—all from Adira.

I began reading the messages:

You are kidding, right!
I have planned so much.
It is your BIRTHDAY!
We have not met since I don't know when . . .

Before I could scroll and read more, the phone started buzzing again. Her number flashed on the screen, and I wondered if I should tell her about the unpleasant situation I was in. I did not want to lie, but discussing my motions with the girl I had recently started dating did not sound like an excellent idea and could hamper the relationship in the longer run. To tell or not to say a word about it was the dilemma.

No secrets, no lies—this was the first promise we made when we started dating.

I cursed the biryani and the tiffin-wallah aunty, but what was done was done. My birthday and all our plans for the day went down the drain, or down the toilet to be more specific. I did not want to make it worse by lying to Adira and feeling guilty about breaking the promise. *But how could I tell her?* It is so embarrassing that girls prefer not to talk about this stuff, I guess. The calls kept coming, and message bombs dropped one after the other, indicating her changes of mood and making it difficult for me to concentrate on what to say, especially with my rumbling intestines which had almost given up on retaining even water for more than a couple of minutes. Later, judging by her messages, I realized her emotions quickly changed from disappointment to anger to frustration, and finally escalated to worry all within five minutes of receiving my message. I was losing strength as well as my thinking abilities with every passing minute.

Finally, when Adira took a break from her mobile terror activities, I took another loo break, after which I typed a small, to-the-point but dirty message. My first dirty message to her was messier than I had hoped it to be.

Upset stomach (read watery). Can't meet. Sorry (sad face).

I was not expecting any more calls or messages from her; not that day, not ever. Now when I think of it, I could have been more subtle in describing my personal circumstances to her—the description was not needed. But at that moment, I thought it was imperative to add the narrative as it added truthfulness to the message and made the truth more believable. Nevertheless, the phone calls stopped, and I was now bothered only about my bathroom visits.

Unfortunately, I could not find the needed medicine in the box where my mother usually keeps all the over-the-counter medicines. Because of the time difference between Delhi and London, I did not think that it was wise to bother my mother with my small troubles, that too when my sister was due to give birth any moment. My health woes were trivial compared to her situation. Also, I did not want my mother to unnecessarily worry about me when she could not do anything about it. As it was a Sunday, neither Rohit nor Piyush answered any of my desperate phone calls. 'Bastards!' I muttered as I picked myself up from the sofa and headed towards the same place in the house once again. The way my strength was leaving my body, I was sure that the next time I would be scooping my body off the floor.

My maid was on leave that day as well. I had given her a day off as I expected to spend the entire day with Adira. Surprisingly, at 1 p.m., my doorbell rang. *Maybe a courier or Amazon delivery*, I contemplated whether I could ask the delivery guy to bring me a few tablets from the nearby medical shop, out of compassion. A small ray of hope bounced its way from my heart to my stomach, or maybe it was just my stomach twisting and turning. I peeped through the keyhole and was shocked by what I saw. Adira stood on the other side of the door with a bag in her hand. I rubbed my tired eyes and opened the door in a jiffy to find her smiling back at me like a mischievous kid.

'How are you now?' she asked me, stepping in. I do not recall who closed the door behind her. Maybe she closed it, or the wind, or it could have been me. I was stunned to see her there and embarrassed to be seen in my miserable condition, almost lifeless. I said nothing but wondered how many ladies in the neighbourhood had seen her standing there as she rang the bell and then walked into the house. The entire block was aware that my family was away, and I did not want any scandal for her. I wanted her to be my wife one day—yes, I did. Even though we had not been together very long, that could not come in the way of my dreaming or wanting something far ahead in the future. I also wondered how long I had before one of the sweet neighbours phoned my mother, who was probably worked up as her daughter was in labour, to tell her that her son had welcomed a beautiful girl in the house and that they were both alone, doing all sorts of unthinkable things. Most likely, it would not be long before the news was wired from Delhi to London at lightning speed.

My train of thoughts was derailed as Adira put her hand on my forehead to check if I had a fever. 'Your temperature seems fine,' she said, removing her warm hand. 'Have you eaten anything?' she asked me, looking at my face with concern in her eyes. I must have looked a mess; the look on her face told me so.

'I had the biryani which is the root cause of my problem,' I tried to force a smile as I answered, but neither of us found my response amusing. 'And some tea,' I added.

'Here, take this with only one sip of water, and then wait for fifteen minutes before you drink or eat anything,' she ordered, handing me a glass with very little water in it and a tablet which I shall not name but was really glad that she had brought with her. I followed her instructions and fifteen minutes later had some liquid to reinstate the lost water.

'I will be in the kitchen,' she told me as she headed out, and I drifted into a tired slumber, fully aware of my surroundings. When I woke up, I was feeling much better.

I had a little rice porridge that Adira had made for the two of us, took a much-needed shower and crashed on the bed again. This time around, I had a much better sleep. I woke up at 9 p.m., feeling much better than I had felt when Adira had walked into the house with the medicines. I looked for Adira and found her in my father's study. She was reading one of his books—an autobiography of a historian.

'Do you always read such boring books?' I broke her concentration with my question, and she looked up from the book instantly.

'I read whatever I get my hands on—a book, the newspaper, a children's book, even a map,' she replied, and chuckled as she adjusted her reading glasses. 'How are you feeling now? Shall I make you something to eat?' her concern for my health was overwhelming.

'Have you eaten anything?' I asked her, and as expected, she had not eaten anything substantial. 'Maggi, then,' I said, and we headed towards the kitchen to make one packet of Maggi noodles for her and khichri for me.

That day I realized that the simplest of tasks, like cooking, can be so much fun if you have the right company. The food turned out to be nice and so did our conversation at the dinner table. That was when she gave me a gift—a watch. 'This is to remind you of all the lovely times we have had together and for all the amazing times that we shall spend in each other's company,' she told me, strapping the brown leather strap around my wrist which had lost considerable volume thanks to the rumble in my stomach for the past many hours. I thanked her for such a thoughtful present. It is still the most memorable gift I have ever received. A mechanical watch which will live forever, just like our love.

Let me confess that I was initially embarrassed in her company, but she warmly made me forget that horrible day. Her jokes and laughter made my birthday special. I asked her if she knew how many ladies had seen her walking in. 'None, but even if they had, why do you care?' she asked, wondering why I was so concerned about what people thought. I could not explain it to her. But it was indeed true that no one had seen her come into my house, or my phone would have been plagued with messages from all my relatives asking me about the girl who came over when Mummy was not home. It was quite late at night, and I decided to drop her back to her house early the next morning before the maid came for her daily duties. I think because I was not feeling or looking very well, Adira did not insist on going back home that night either.

After food, as Adira talked about her brave journey alone to my home and how I looked as if I were dying that morning, my phone rang. It was my mother. I answered the call and heard the best words I had ever heard in my life—I had become an uncle! My niece was healthy and looked like me. At least that is what my mother thought at that moment.

The phone call lasted a few minutes, after which Adira and I celebrated the good news with a few spoonfuls of chocolate ice cream from the freezer. It was 12 a.m., and though I was free the next day, Adira had to work, so we decided to call it a day. I offered her my nightclothes which she politely refused. 'You can sleep in my parents' room,' I told her, but surprisingly, she joined me in my bedroom instead.

'I am going to sleep here because you are not well and might need me at night, but do not get any other ideas,' she warned me as she walked in. 'Moreover, my mother can call you any time, remember?' she added cheekily, and resumed reading the book with her glasses on.

'Goodnight,' I whispered, sliding under the sheets and smiling. We shared the same bed that night, and I hoped to share my life with her.

Thinking about how my plans for the day had yet again been spoilt by fate, for better or for worse—I drifted off into the world of dreams.

22 JULY 2018

Although we had discussed it earlier, neither of us woke up before my housemaid came.

'Oh no!' I exclaimed, getting out of bed as I was awakened by the doorbell. Shanti was the least hard-working maid I had ever known. She was usually late for work, apart from a few occasions, and today was one of them. She superficially cleaned the floor and never dusted anything. She ignored all the instructions my mother ever gave her, and she broke more plates than she cleaned. However, she was the only maid who was willing to work in a house with a young, unmarried man—me. She had been coming to our house since we were both kids, and she saw me as an elder brother. Also, she charged a little less than the others.

The main reason why she had maintained her employment in our house was the fact that she knew everything that happened in the homes in the neighbourhood and was my mother's personal news agency. Like most housewives, my mother wanted to be aware of what was cooking in the other people's kitchens and lives. Shanti, unlike her name, was never *shant* or quiet. She was the Ashanti of our neighbourhood.

The ringing doorbell sounded like a siren, and it felt as if I were being raided by moral police for being alone with a girl in my own house. I sprang out of bed and looked at Adira who was still asleep. 'Great!' I recall saying, but I cannot remember why I said it. I bolted the door behind me, tucked my T-shirt in, and contemplated whether letting the chatterbox into the house at all was a good idea. I cared too much about what people would say or think back then, and despite the house being in a mess, with the sink full of dirty dishes from last night and before, and a layer of dust on top of the floor under my slippers—I decided to give her the day off.

'*Aaj chutti, kal ana* (take a day off and come tomorrow),' I told her, peeking from the side of the main gate, not meeting her eyes just in case if she could read people's minds to find their hidden secrets to meet her daily requirement of gossip.

'*Kyun* (why)?' she asked, reinforcing my belief.

'Because there are no dirty dishes and I cleaned the floor just before you rang the bell,' I lied outright, and unexpectedly, she believed me. Muttering something about my failure at not informing her on time and wasting more than a few hours of her time, she turned on her heels and off she went towards her next destination.

I hurried back in and bolted the door behind me. My stomach was rumbling again, and I could not figure out if it was asking for food or going to give me more trouble. It was 9.30 a.m., and Adira was still sleeping. *Must have been reading all night long!* I knew that she was a night owl and loved to bury herself in a good book. *It is quite a sunny day, and there are so many people out on the street already. How on earth am I going to sneak her out of the house?* I decided to think about it in the bathroom.

When I came out, I was not feeling that great, but Adira had to go to work that day. So, I gathered all the strength that was left in me and opened the door to wake her up. She was awake and looked surprised as I entered the room.

'You locked me in your room? Why?' she asked me sternly, but her face changed expressions looking at my state. I flopped on the bed and blinked my eyes twice.

'Let me drop you back home so that you can go to work,' I said before resting my head against the headboard.

'You are not well, and I am not leaving you alone. We need to see a doctor,' she declared, and started typing on her phone. I was too drained to argue with her or even ask her what she was doing on the phone. I sat back as she called a few people: her boss, her maid, Tamanna, a doctor.

'Let's go,' she said, stretching out her hand.

'Where?' I almost knew the answer.

'To a doctor, where else?'

She has seen me in a condition in which I would hate to look at myself in the mirror, and she has not run away yet. I don't think she will run away now. She has been so caring and loving. I was worried that she would be disgusted by me and my ailment. Instead, she stood by me, cooked for me, took care of me; and now she is taking me to a doctor. Who gets a girl like that nowadays? I wondered, as pride and happiness filled my heart even in the painful condition that I was in.

'You can't go out of the house in broad daylight,' I told her in a shaky voice, but she chose to ignore my free advice.

'Let's go,' she repeated, almost looming over me.

'I do not want people to talk,' I told her.

'People who have time to talk about others are not important enough to be concerned about. Moreover, I have called Tamanna over. She will park her car outside, and we can both go with her without many tongues wagging . . .' I lost her there. My stomach was at it again, and this time the pain was so intense that I passed out.

When I woke up, I was in hospital with an IV drip attached to my arm. Tamanna, Piyush and Adira were around me. The doctors thought that it was a blend of some bug and food poisoning. I was to be admitted into hospital for two days. Piyush and Adira took turns to be with me. Piyush had called my mother who was happy to know that they were all by my side.

A lot of people remember things from the time that they spend in hospital but not me. All I know is that Adira was next to me every time I woke up. She came back with me when I was discharged and under the care of Piyush's family for the rest of the week. The love, dedication and care that I saw in her eyes are all that come back to me when I try to recall the two days on that hospital bed.

She, however, remembered more, and later she told me how I was behaving like a child and did not let any nurse inject me or change the IV needle I had managed to rip off, or even my clothes.

31 JULY 2018

I had completely recovered and was grateful to God for the girl who stood by me. My sister and her baby were doing fine too. I received a daily update from my mother about their well-being. A video chat with my niece was an everyday activity for me now. I missed being with my family when they were having such a great time. My parents had extended their stay till September, and then my sister, her husband and the newest addition to their near-perfect family were due to make a trip to India with my parents. I was excited at the thought of meeting them all.

While I was still at the hospital, Piyush's mother called mine. I was shocked when I had the phone shoved into my face as soon as I woke up. My mother was on a video call with Piyush, worried sick, sitting miles away from me and sobbing like a child. 'I am going to be okay, Mummy,' I recall telling her but she wouldn't stop crying.

Thankfully, Tamanna intervened and took the phone away to tell her that I was way better than I looked, not forgetting to assure her that I was in safe hands, Adira's hands, and thus began my mother's love relationship with the girl who stole my heart. Within hours of my conversation with her, my mother had slyly found out all that she could about Adira through relatives—mainly Tamanna's parents. She later declared that she found her 'agreeable enough'. I knew she was lying, she knew that Adira was my perfect match. After that day, during every conversation, Mummy remembered to talk about Adira and how she would love to meet the girl who had taken such good care of me in her absence. 'She is just a friend,' I told my mother every time we talked, an unnecessary explanation which gave me away. No matter how smart you think you are, when you fall in love, your mother is the first one who gets to know. I believe mothers sniff out love affairs, and mine could smell the fragrance of love in my life despite being thousands of miles away from me.

Every time Mummy reminded me of her anticipated meeting with Adira, I wondered how Adira would be as a daughter-in-law. We had recently started dating, but I knew that she was the only one I ever wanted to be with. By then we had started talking a little about the future and how we saw our life five years down the line. She wanted to have kids—three kids, she had declared just last night when we were texting.

Do you like kids? she asked me. Did I like kids? I did, but did I fancy the idea of kids of my own? I had not given it much thought until then.

Maybe, I replied honestly, and my honesty irked her.

So, you do not like kids? she was putting words in my mouth.

I never said that I do not like them! I spoke in my defence. I like kids, I love my sister's baby even before I have met her. But I have not thought about my kids as such. I didn't know how to explain it better to her.

K, came her reply, and that was that. This was something that was bothering me a lot. Every time we had an argument or a disagreement, or if one did not like anything about the other, she used to go silent, or respond in monosyllables, sometimes even sounds—hmmm . . . ah . . . oh . . . what kind of a response was this?

Adira had gone quiet after our talk about our imaginary kids, and I decided to meet her and cheer her up.

Half an hour after I left home, I stood outside her building. She requested the guard to let me in. I had gone there after many months. The last time I was there, her mother had called. I had avoided going to her place since, and I usually dropped her at the main gate after our dates. *There is no need to be scared*, I told my troubled heart, and took the elevator to her floor.

She was waiting for me in the corridor dressed in a white off-the-shoulder dress, looking divine as always. She hugged me hard and took me into her house, holding my hand very tightly. Her smile and the warmth of her skin as it touched mine felt like home. In a comforting sort of way she was all that I ever needed.

Her house was the same as I remembered it to be apart from a photo frame in the living room with a framed picture of her parents, in their happy times.

'What do you want to have? Tea?' she asked me, smiling, and I could think of nothing else but her. I picked her up in my arms and carried her into her room as she giggled against my chest.

NEXT THREE WEEKS—THAT WENT BY IN A HEARTBEAT . . .

We kept meeting each other more often, mostly at my house. I was getting comfortable meeting her at her home too, but after she told me that the house belonged to her mother's best friend who lived only a few kilometres away, I decided to maintain my distance. I used to sneak Adira into my house after sunset, not that I had never taken her home during the daytime, but we usually met after work on Fridays and had dinner somewhere. I gave my maid time off from work all weekend. I learnt that Adira was not just a stunner but an excellent cook, apart from her chai which was the least appealing thing that she made in the kitchen. She cooked all my favourite vegetarian dishes, usually singing old Hindi songs. Dressed in my work shirts, in the morning she made breakfast for the two of us as I helped by cleaning the dishes or chopping veggies.

In August she applied for a week of paid leave and stayed over with me every day—she wanted to see how it would be if we were to live together, as loving and living together are not the same thing. We fared quite well as those turned out to be the best days of my life and gave me memories so precious that I would not want to share them with anyone. The time with her made me fall further in love with her, this time madly. She was worried as she did not want to end up like her mother, separated from the man whom she once loved because they were not compatible. I took a week off too and proved to her that we were perfect for each other, just like two pieces of a puzzle. That week also made me see her as my future; she was the one that I could do anything to be with.

We loved, learnt, argued and made up—all of this built the foundation of a very strong friendship. Our relationship was beyond lust, affection and adoration. It was love in its most beautiful form. Every evening when my parents called, she sat opposite me and read her book, smiling at the mention of her name, and I smothered a laugh when my mother teased me and asked me if she should talk to Adira's family. I loved watching her get ready and kissed the Om which was tattooed at the nape of her neck at every opportunity. I did have to visit my office twice for a couple of hours during those seven days, and both times, when I unlocked the door upon my return, I found her humming an old Hindi song and cooking for me. Every time I told her that I loved her, she patted me lovingly on my head and said, 'You are silly.' It was her version of I love you too.

While she stayed with me, whenever we went in or out of the house, I made her sit in the back seat of our car, covered from head to toe in a dark blanket. My concern for her reputation and fear of what people would say had not left me.

We did spend evenings at our balcony, away from the preying eyes of my neighbours. That is my favourite place in the house, and we sat having tea and talking, or planning our lives ahead and discussing our future together. Sometimes we just spent our time sitting intertwined with each other, her legs within mine, holding hands, saying nothing, just absorbing it all. Those were the days when I would click random, candid pictures of hers all evening to freeze the memories so that I could revisit them later. She never really liked the camera in her face and would get angry after a couple of shots. Later, looking at the same shots of hers; she would insist on me to buy a professional camera and make something out of my hobby. It was her way of telling me how beautiful she thought her pictures were. 'Yes, someday I will,' I told her every time, looking at her face as she scanned the pictures with admiration in her eyes.

Every night, as she sat reading in bed, I played with her shiny hair, kissed her forehead and wondered why it had taken us so long to reach where we were. I loved kissing her forehead as she furrowed her brow while reading her novels. She used to be so into them, as if she were one of the characters. Also, those seven days we stayed together, I was a pure vegetarian as she had asked me to try it for a week and if I did not feel lighter and better, I could go back to my 'chicken-eating ways' as she put it. I am still a vegetarian. It was all so perfect that it scared me. When things are so right, something terrible is just lurking around the corner waiting for a chance to come and end it all for you in a single blow.

We did not have to wait long—her mother knew what it took to take my peace of mind away, and she managed to execute her plan very well.

26 AUGUST 2018

My memories of that day are as fresh as this morning's in my mind. It was a Saturday, the Saturday which I wish had never happened in my life. I had changed a lot from the person I was a few months ago, before Adira had fallen in love with me. I was more self-confident and was sure of her feelings towards me. This certainty added an uncalled-for sense of superiority in my behaviour—mostly towards her. She trusted me and gave me the power to hurt her, and I have no pride when I say that I unintentionally exploited that power, more than a few times.

I had mentioned her ex during the last fight we'd had the day before, and that was not the first time I had done that. We were at a coffee shop in Gurgaon when the topic of her mother popped up in the conversation. I was really done with her mother's hatred for me and had gotten into a habit of taunting Adira in my frustration. From the person who once held her hand and made her believe in love again—'Just because of something which happened in the past, do not stop believing in love, do not stop looking for love, do not stop loving.'—I reiterated this to her on numerous occasions, but later I became the boyfriend who blamed her and her mother for everything that happened in the past.

'She does not know how to judge men. She made an error in her own life, and she is determined to screw yours too by telling you to keep a distance from me. You cannot see beyond your mother and her happiness,' I remember saying in a not-so-hushed tone. I was embarrassed as soon as the words left my mouth, but the damage was done. Heads turned towards us, eyes moved, waves of laughter were suppressed, and a few giggles reached our ears. I saw Adira's face lose all its colour. She was the palest I had ever seen her. Her eyes were filled with tears, but none dared to trickle down and show her weakness to the world. She bowed her head and pretended to check her phone. A minute later, she stood up, leaving her coffee at the table. To repay my behaviour that evening, she took an auto and went back to her apartment, alone. My ego was too inflated to go after her and apologize, because it had been a while since I had said sorry to her, even when I was wrong. Adira always forgave me without me asking for forgiveness. She usually allowed me to get away with my mistakes; she was beyond the petty things that were taking me over at a rigorous speed. Whenever we fought, we made up with no apologies from either side. It was like a mutual understanding—one called, and the other could not disconnect. We chatted about what happened without stretching it too far. I was the wrong party, mostly, and all I had to do was to make her smile.

Filled with vain pride and ego, I now know that I had turned into the worst version of myself when life had given me a chance to be with the person I once only dreamt of being with. I did not call her that evening. I was angry at her. Why? One might ask as I was clearly the one who was at fault. Honestly, I do not have any explanation or reason now. Back then, I thought that her mother had been really mean to me and was taking Adira away from me. I wanted to use my anger to tell her how much I disapproved of her disapproval of me. In fact, it was me and my actions that were taking her away from me and maybe also contributing towards her mother's dislike for me. I know better now.

That Saturday, the twenty-sixth, both Adira and I were invited to attend a party hosted by Tamanna and Piyush. They were all set to be parents soon, and before beginning their diaper duties, some six months later, they wanted to let us all know how excited they were.

4.30 p.m.

I reached Piyush's posh house in Gurgaon a little early and waited patiently for Adira to arrive. She did not, and I got worried after waiting for half an hour. I checked with Tamanna, who rightly told me that I should be the one to know about Adira's recent whereabouts and not her. I was confident that she was aware of even the small rifts between Adira and me in the recent past, and being Adira's friend, she was by default at her side and not mine.

Finally, Adira walked in, with a few of her friends. She did not have a car, or any other ride, and Gurgaon is quite far away from Noida. I always picked her up and dropped her to places, even on weekdays, but that evening I did not check how she would manage to get there on her own. She had always been an independent girl and could very well commute on her own, but I had always felt it was my responsibility to be by her side, to ensure that her travels and commutes were safe.

But not that day, because I was becoming more and more of an arsehole every day. Resorting to childish ways to make her realize my importance is one of the things that today I am not very proud of. The other mistakes include taking her for granted, not prioritizing her happiness and not thinking beyond what I wanted. At that stage of our relationship, it was all about me, my ego and my self-appraised value.

As I wanted, expected and hoped, Adira walked straight up to me after greeting the hosts. Despite the public spectacle that I had made of her at the coffee shop, she held my hand warmly and stood next to me as if nothing had happened. Piyush, Rohit, I and another friend of ours, Rishabh, stood sipping our drinks.

'How did you come?' I asked her shamelessly a little while later.

'Uber,' she gave me a look I was unable to decode. *Is she fed up with me? Or does she want to know what am I feeling? Can she still read me like a book? Does she still look into my soul with her eyes?*

'About last evening . . .' She began, and I interrupted her.

'Let's not talk about it, please, not here at least.' I was the arsehole who did not want to apologize or even discuss the topic as I knew very well that I was at fault. Avoidance was my sole purpose.

'Okay. But we need to talk,' she told me, looking directly into my eyes, and I felt her arms shaking slightly as she held my left arm with both of her hands.

'Sure, but why now?' I asked her, surprised, as we usually reserved our private conversations to our secret places, mostly at either of our homes.

'It is important,' she told me in a serious undertone, and we headed towards the balcony.

Piyush and Tamanna's house was on the thirtieth floor. It was a lavish penthouse gifted by Piyush's dad to his son, yet it looked quite cramped with all the people in it. Piyush and Tamanna had invited all their friends and co-workers. The place was buzzing with conversations and laughter, and the balcony was the only place where we could spend some time alone as it was still sunny outside and no one dared to leave the comfortable, cool house and stand in the balcony.

I closed the glass door behind us, and suddenly it all went so quiet. The sun was directly in my eyes, so I quickly moved towards the chairs in the corner which were luckily under the shade of a few plants in the balcony. Adira quietly followed me, waiting for me to settle down before she said what she had to say.

'Tell me,' I said, sipping my drink which I had carried with me.

'Sit down, it is something important,' she paused, and adjusted the hem of her dress as both of us took our seats opposite each other.

'I need to know where this is headed, Ronnie,' she said.

'What do you mean? Where is what headed?' I went back to the fight yesterday evening in my head and tried to make sense of her question.

'Where are we headed? Where is this relationship going? What is next for us?' she drew a deep breath as she said the last bit.

I had wanted to talk to her about our future myself. My parents were coming back soon. And with almost all my friends and cousins settled into family life or enjoying matrimonial bliss, I too wanted to move forward. Marriage was the next step, of course, but her mother, with her resentment towards everything that I had done to win her over, was driving me nuts. This was probably one of the many reasons why I was so insecure about Adira too, and I took it all out on her, not that I am defending my actions but I know that there were many underlying reasons behind the change in my behaviour, and this was one of the most critical ones.

'What do you want next for us?' I was honestly nervous to talk about the 'M' word, but it had been the elephant in the room for quite a while, and the sooner we addressed it, the better.

'Whatever you want, really,' she must have been quite unsure of what I was thinking to have said this. Maybe it was the fight a night ago or my indifference towards the topic.

'I want to get married.' There, I said it, and I waited for her reaction.

'To whom?' she asked me with the most innocent expression on her face, and I realized how little she knew about my feelings for her. I felt some guilt too for not opening up to her recently.

'To you, who else? I've wanted to get married to you all along but your mother . . .' Before I could say more, she sealed my lips with hers, and I got an answer to my rather unromantic marriage proposal. She said, 'Yes'! And then she cried a little, drenching my floral shirt around the shoulders with her tears.

'What are these tears for?' I asked her teasingly.

'For yesterday evening . . . . I thought that you had stopped loving me . . .' This time I had to shut her up with a kiss, and we let bygones be bygones.

'Come, let us go inside, or Tamanna will wonder where we are,' I said after a moment of silence, but Adira wanted to tell me something more. She held my hand and made me sit in the same place again before she began talking.

'Listen, my mother's opinion matters a lot to me.' *There we go again,* I thought, and rolled my eyes at her, knowing that this irritated her the most.

'Can you not do that please?' she scolded me rather severely and resumed. 'So, I spoke to Mamma about us last night after our fight. She says that she has found a guy for me.' Her statement filled me with more anger for her mother. The one thing that had done more damage than anything her mother had ever said or done was my unnecessary anger, which usually had no solid foundation whatsoever.

'Really? Again?' I mocked her mother and her choice in men at every given opportunity and was at it again, 'Remember the last guy she found for you?' I reminded her rather cruelly.

'Can we not go there, please? I have something to tell you. We have . . . I mean my mother and I have come to an agreement,' she said, choosing her words very carefully.

'Agreement?' I really wanted to know where all this was headed.

'Yes, so . . . listen to me with a calm head, okay. I have told Mamma that I love you,' she gave me a reassuring smile and continued. 'My mother thinks that I am mad and says this is because I have not yet met any decent guys in my life. She does not understand jobs and a simple life. She is more of a business and farmhouses kind of a person . . . you know what I mean, right?'

I chose not to react as I wanted to hear her to the end, say no to the agreement, whatever it was, and present my condition in front of Adira. *Tell her to choose her mother or me, and walk back into the party*, my head was bursting with anger.

'So, I told her, "Fine. I will meet the guy that you have chosen for me, and if I do not like him let me be with Ronnie,"' she beamed at me, and that was it.

I lost control of my anger.

'What! You have agreed to meet other men!' I failed to understand why she was so happy about this stupid solution of hers. She'd agreed to meet other men to please her mother! She did not for once think how I would feel about it.

All I remember from the next moment is that my right hand went under the plastic table between us, which had two glasses on it, and I overturned the table. The glasses flew in the air and hit the ground, smashing into tiny pieces that could hurt someone, prick them and make them bleed, just like her words had pricked and wounded my heart.

'Enough of you and your mother now. Go and get married to the guy she has chosen for you and do not bother to tell me where and when. You are dead for me now,' I said, standing up and not bothering about the mess I had made in someone else's balcony. 'In fact . . . you know what . . . send me an invite to your wedding. I shall be there and see someone spoil their life by getting married to the girl who cannot think beyond her mother!' the devil had possessed me, and I was talking nothing but shit.

'It is just a meeting, Ronnie . . . and . . . and then she will see that I am not going to fall for any other guy . . . don't you see?' she started sobbing uncontrollably.

'No, I do not see anything. What is the guarantee that you will not fall in love with this guy's money, to say the least?' that blow was way below the belt, but I did not care. For I was fighting with her mom and not her. I could not see Adira standing in front of me. I only saw her mother there, and all the venom was for her. The balcony door opened, and Tamanna walked in to confront us, or me to be more specific. She looked at all the broken glass with horror and immediately went to hug her friend.

'Has he hit you, Adira?' she asked her sobbing friend.

Great! So now I am a woman beater. What do these women in Adira's life think of me? Why am I such a monster for them?

Adira moved her head slowly, signalling a no, and Tamanna took her in, holding her tightly in her arms as if I were an armed terrorist. On their way back into the house, Tamanna stared at me as if she was going to burn me to ashes with her stare. Moments later, Rohit came out to talk to me, and Piyush followed. I told them it was a small fight which had escalated quickly and that there was no need to panic. The sun was setting. I saw it disappear behind the tall building and then joined the group inside to drink and pass out. It was turning into the worst night of my life.

10.30 p.m.

I had had way too many drinks that evening, and the world was finally a happy place again. Most people were more than a few pegs down, and we were all merrily talking about stuff that did not matter to any of us or to anyone else in the world and would be conveniently forgotten the next day. I expected Adira to go back home at around 9 p.m. as she usually slipped out of parties to be back home by 10 p.m. She stayed around her group of friends and Tamanna all through the night. Her friends stuck to her like hawks, protecting her from me. Finally, as people began dispersing, she walked up to me to ask if I could drop her home.

'I am not driving,' I told her rudely.

'I know. We can take an Uber and go to your place. Tomorrow is Sunday, and we can talk about all this tomorrow, alone,' she suggested politely.

'There is no need to talk now. You are dead for me,' I remember telling her, and I observed her face to see her reaction. She was unbelievably quiet and repeated her request to accompany me back home.

'I told you—you are dead to me,' I repeated the words that still haunt me.

'Come, Adira, you are not going anywhere tonight. Stay with us,' Tamanna interrupted our heated conversation. 'He has lost his mind. He does not deserve you!' she added. I mocked her once she turned her back at me. Rohit hit me with a newspaper on my head, and I remembered that she was also my sister-in-law and my behaviour with her was entirely improper.

'I shall head back home, actually. I will take an Uber,' Adira told her friend calmly, and started tapping on her phone to open the app.

'No, don't take a cab at this hour. I will tell Piyush to drop you,' Tamanna instructed her, and left to go and look for her husband.

'Come home,' she said, placing her hand on my hand with such sadness in her eyes that it cannot be described in words. I felt nothing. Her feelings did not reach my stubborn soul. I picked up my drink, jerked my hand away, and did not look back at her even once till she finally got up to leave.

One of Piyush's friends and his wife, who lived in Noida, were leaving the party and had happily offered to drop Adira back home. I was relieved to know that she was not taking a cab but was still angry with her. One by one, all the drinkers left my side, and I sat drinking alone. Later, it dawned on me that I had overreacted. But I would not apologize or accept that I was at fault. I knew that in the morning she would call me. It was a Sunday, and I would see her. We would make up, I knew. *And it is not too bad, come to think of it. If she meets this guy once and says she does not like him, her mother will have no objection to her marrying me. It is more comfortable than going against her wishes and seeing Adira sulk all her life*, I thought. 'Let me wait till tomorrow's call then,' I said to no one in particular.

Fifteen minutes later, I was all set to head back home with Rohit and his fiancée. There was one more guy who was to accompany us in the car. He was a non-drinker and was our chauffeur for the evening.

11.45 p.m.

We had just got out of the building and taken a left turn when a speeding truck zoomed past us. Our driver who was not drunk could not manage the vehicle, and we almost crashed into the divider. 'What the heck, man!' Rohit screamed loudly at the guy whose name was Taran.

'He came out of nowhere, and he was driving in the wrong side of the road. Trucks should not be here. It is a residential area,' Taran explained, and we all knew that he was right. The truck had come out of nowhere and was not even supposed to be on that road. But in that one moment of panic and fear, my entire life flashed in front of me, and I realized the obvious—the importance of life and the reckless way it could be gone in seconds. I was shaken and could not utter a single word for a very long time. Taran got down to check the damage to the car. There were a few scratches, and one of the tyres needed to be changed before we could move on.

'Has anyone noted down the registration number of the truck?' I asked while Taran changed the tyre on the deserted road. No one had, even when we should have. Ten minutes later, we were on the road again, this time very cautiously.

We had not gone very far when we saw another car that was smashed into the divider. The two front seats were almost squashed, and there was blood everywhere. There were no people around, but looking at the car it was clear that it was a recent accident, and maybe the survivors or the victims were still in the car.

'Maybe it was the same truck that caused this accident. It was driving in the wrong lane,' Taran said to no one in particular. The car was badly damaged in the accident. Taran slowed down as we drove past the golden Maruti Zen.

'What are you doing?' Rohit asked Taran when he didn't hit the brakes to see if there were any survivors. Looking at the condition of the car, it was difficult to imagine that there were any. Witnessing the amount of blood in and out of the car we were all scared. Upon Rohit's insistence, Taran stopped the car, we were twenty steps or more away from it then.

'There might be people in there,' Sagarika uttered in a barely audible voice as she turned her head to inspect the horrific sight. She was the first one to open the door. Slowly she got down from the car.

'Get back in here,' Taran ordered her. He got out and pulled her back into the car. He came and sat behind the driver's seat and locked the car doors so that no one could step out of the vehicle again.

'We need to help them!' she protested, and looked at Rohit and me.

'Yes, we must,' Rohit said, and I gave my unsaid vote to them. I was too scared to do anything and too drunk to utter something sensible.

'Are you guys crazy? When you admit them in the hospital, the police will lock us all up. I have seen this happen to my uncle. No one is getting down. Rohit, you are drunk and so is Ronnie. The police are known to create false cases and extract money. I do not think anyone could have survived in that car. Look at it. Why invite trouble?' Taran hushed everyone. Before we could think or do anything, we were on the move. Sagarika pleaded with him one more time to just go and see if there was someone we could save, but Taran was adamant. I turned around to look at the wreckage for any signs of a survivor. It was badly smashed in the front. 'No one would have survived. They would not have been wearing seat belts. It is not uncommon to find people not wearing seat belts while driving in India, especially when there was no one around to check or fine them. Seat belts are not about safety but looked down upon as an imposition that cause nothing but inconvenience to people On top of that, the safety standards of small cars are appalling. Most small cars do not come with airbags in India,' I stated the obvious absent-mindedly, and we left the scene with memories to haunt us forever.

I was dropped home first. Despite being heavily drunk, I could not sleep. The scene of the car accident and the sensations of our own crash kept waking me up. I was sorry for the people who had lost their lives. Finally, at 2 a.m., I decided to apologize to Adira for being so rude to her, for hurting her. I wanted to begin afresh, so I typed a WhatsApp message:

> I am so sorry, Baby, please forgive me. We will do as you want and see how it goes. I am sorry for everything I said about your mother too. Love you. I wish you were here with me.

I pressed the send button and waited for it to deliver. It did, and two grey ticks appeared which never turned blue.

27 AUGUST 2018

I woke up at 9.30 a.m. The maid had called in sick the day before, and I did not expect her to return for a week. Like clockwork, I sat up, rubbed my eyes and typed the customary 'good morning' text to Adira. My message from last night had not been read yet. *She must have slept late last night*, I told myself. It was Sunday, and I had a very important meeting to discuss a start-up idea with a potential investor. I had to go and meet them at a mall in Gurgaon. I was really looking forward to it as it would kick-start my entrepreneurial dreams. I had kept it a secret from Adira as I wanted to surprise her, and her mother, who wished to marry her daughter to a businessman. So, without giving Adira's absence much thought, I began my daily activities and prepared for the hectic day ahead. I was out of my house and in a cab at 10 a.m. sharp, and reached Gurgaon on time. I had checked my phone a zillion times to see if she had read my message, only to be disappointed every time with the same grey ticks next to my messages. The recollection of the fatal accident came in front of my eyes many times, and each time that happened I thanked the Almighty for my life, and also for the ones around me. It was an ugly sight to remember or describe to anyone.

Because of my clear recollection of the events the night before, which included my fight with Adira, the nasty things I had said in my rage that were uncalled for, and the condition of the car which horrified me more than anything had ever seen before, I valued the lives of all my loved ones and felt terribly sorry for all my actions. I had realized how valuable human life is, and how a stupid action can make one lose all, in a matter of seconds. I could not concentrate on my meeting that morning, and I dialled Adira's number a few times to say sorry, but in vain. She did not pick up my calls. I could not blame her for acting that way. I knew if I had been in her place, I would have reacted in a worse manner.

When there was no response from her by 11 a.m., I decided to call one of Adira's colleagues who lived in the same apartment building and ask her to put Adira on the phone—cheap move? I know, but the trick worked each time she stopped picking my calls. She never wanted me to involve anyone else in our fights, and the moment I did, she gave me a chance to explain myself. So, I called Swati—her work buddy. She told me that she was not at home and was heading out of town. 'Thanks,' I said, before disconnecting the call. I formulated a plan to surprise her.

I took the cab back home, picked up my bike, got a bouquet of white roses and a box of chocolates from a nearby florist, and reached her building at around 3 p.m. It was a dull, grey day. Monsoon clouds had covered the sky like a thick blanket, and the sun was unable to shine through. Now, when I recall the afternoon, I can even describe it as a rather gloomy and sad day. One could see birds returning to their nests in large batches, way before their usual time. The sound of dusty wind echoed everywhere, and an odd drop of rain fell on me time and again, reminding me of the uncertainty of the weather.

I had parked my bike at the designated visitor parking and was walking towards the entry gate when my phone rang. *Shall I tell her that I am here?* I contemplated as I fished my phone out of my pocket. *Maybe not. Let it be a surprise.* I had expected a call from Adira, but it was actually Piyush. I had not called him last night to inform him about my safe return to the house, which was customary after a party at his home. I skipped his call as I had a more important matter to attend to. I sent him a message instead: Busy, will call later.

Piyush is the type who always respects a person's privacy, no matter who that person is. I cannot say that about any other relative of mine, but Piyush has been like that ever since I've known him. Surprisingly, I got another call from him despite my text message. I wondered if he had not yet seen my message and disconnected the call again, but then he called me a third time, within seconds of my disconnecting his call. Knowing what kind of person he is, I sensed that it must have been something critical. I was in the lift, and usually, the reception is pretty bad when the elevator goes up or down. Still, I answered his call.

'Hello?'

'Where are you?' Piyush asked me, and from his tone I could imagine his face all flustered and drained.

'At Adira's house. Is everything all right?' Tamanna was pregnant then, and my mind worked in different directions, throwing ill thoughts about her, at me. 'Is Tamanna okay?' I asked instantly without giving him any time to respond to my first question.

'Why are you at her house?' Piyush asked me, and then he said, 'Tamanna is fine. Listen, Ronnie . . .' his voice started breaking up.

'I cannot hear you,' I told him, wondering if he could hear me.

'Listen . . . Ronnie . . . we . . . You must . . . mother . . . hospital . . . Gurgaon.' This was all that I could hear before the call was disconnected.

I got out of the lift as soon as it opened without realizing that I was two floors away from Adira's floor and someone had pressed the buttons to get into the elevator.

'Oh my God!' I exclaimed way too loudly, and embarrassed myself in front of an elderly couple who were just coming out of their house when I realized my mistake, but by then the lift doors had closed behind me.

I decided to deal with one thing at a time and dialled Piyush's number to know what had happened and whose mother was in hospital. I feared that it was either Piyush's or Tamanna's mother. The call went on voicemail as he was trying to get connected to someone, most likely me because as soon as I disconnected the call, my phone had Piyush's incoming call on it.

'Sorry about that, I was in the lift. What happened?' I asked him as calmly as I could.

'Listen to me very carefully . . .' he began, and the rest of his words made my world crumble into pieces.

ARTEMIS HOSPITAL, GURGAON

27 AUGUST 2017

Piyush did not give me any particulars. He just told me that Adira was hurt. How badly? He could not tell me. It was worrying to not know as hurt could be anything from a scratch to a fracture to a life-threatening injury. I was terrified and my heart was palpitating. Unfit to drive all the way from Noida to Gurgaon, I wanted someone to pick me up and take me to her. A cab would have taken forever to arrive, and as it was getting close to peak traffic hours, it would have been caught in traffic all evening. A bike ride was the quickest option for me, but in my present situation it was definitely not the safest.

Suddenly, it was as if I heard Adira, 'Ronnie, come on! It is just a bike ride!' She had a habit of saying this, mocking my fear for her safety when she asked me to take her out for a drive after 12 a.m. on Delhi roads. I did not find Delhi very safe to roam around with her after dark.

My mind was playing games with me, but this time I knew that it was in my own interest. I had to go to her. She needed me then more than she had ever needed me. Fifteen minutes later, I was on my way to be by her side. My mind was occupied with all sorts of thoughts and worries, yet my body was in control. The worst times tell you how strong you are, and that was the time which tested my strength.

I parked outside the hospital at 6.30 p.m. and called Piyush straight away. He had gone back home to check on Tamanna who could not come to the hospital despite wanting to see her best friend. 'Her mother is there,' Piyush informed me.

'Oh, okay,' I was not expecting her mother to come over for a minor injury and my fears worsened. 'How badly is she hurt? Where is she?' I inquired, walking down the corridor that leads to the outpatient department.

'She is in the ICU,' he finally told me, and that is when I realized that all my worst fears had come true. She was in the ICU, and her mother had come from Chandigarh to see her. She had met with an accident the night we went to the party at Tamanna and Piyush's house and was severely injured. She was unconscious when I saw her through the glass window in the ICU. I could not see her face, for she was surrounded by machines that were blinking, I knew a blinking device was a good sign; it meant that she was there, resting, recovering, fighting and not losing the battle. As it was after 6 p.m., I was not allowed to go in and see her till the next day.

Piyush joined Adira's mother and me in the hospital a few hours later. While I sat alone with her mother, I did not dare to ask her if she knew how it had happened and what her daughter's condition was. I was not scared of what she would think or say about me, or if she would be rude to me or scold me for having dated her daughter without her approval. It was way beyond the petty fight of likes and dislikes—it was the look in her eyes. Every time a doctor spoke about her baby daughter who was lying unconscious on the bed inside a room where we could not even enter at that hour, her ghostly eyes hovered over to the door—expressionless. She had tears in them, but none trickled down, and this made my guilt deeper, deep enough to penetrate my soul.

Adira is a strong girl, and that day I found out where she got her strength from. Her mother loved Adira more than I could even imagine loving her. Adira was all that she had in the world. She was her only child. The human she had created and loved all those years—she made her the person I fell in love with. I was so selfish and cruel in saying that Adira would have to choose between her mother and me. I wondered if it was all too late now. I felt like a beast, sitting across from her; a monster who tried to take her beloved daughter away from her by emotionally blackmailing her.

I asked Piyush how and what had happened but not in front of her mother, as I did not want to increase her pain. She had so far borne my presence there, for the sake of her daughter—I knew that, and I tried to be kind to her, for Adira.

The vehicle in which Adira and Piyush's friends had set off towards Noida after the party had met with an accident. No one knew how and with what the car had collided, but it was severely damaged. The couple, who were seated in the front, had lost their lives. Adira had been in a coma ever since she was brought to the hospital in the morning. I immediately knew that the car which we had seen, a Zen, was theirs. *I was there, and I did not help her!* The recollection of this fact still kills me. The accident was reported early in the morning by a passer-by who had managed to bring all three to the hospital in an auto. By then, Adira had lost a lot of blood and the other two travellers in the car had been declared—brought dead.

'Could they have been saved? The couple?' I asked Piyush.

He did not know. Maybe they could have been saved had I not listened to Taran. I felt so small! We did not even go close to the car as we were worried about some hypothetical court cases. Probably, Adira would have also not gone into a coma had she received timely care and medical attention, had we not been the cowardly jerks that we had been.

Adira had a broken hand and two broken ribs as she was not wearing a seat belt. She had also suffered a brain injury, but as there was quite a lot of swelling around the brain, the doctors were not able to determine how long it would take to heal properly so they could tell us what had actually gone wrong or why she was unable to regain consciousness and was in a coma.

PRESENT TIME

CHANDIGARH, INDIA

Every weekend, I visit her at her mother's home in Chandigarh. Adira, though, doesn't remember me. She doesn't know who she is to me; she has no recollection of the memorable time we spent in each other's company; she doesn't even remember my last visit to her which was only a week ago, as she doesn't remember herself.

It has been a little over one year since the accident, and she still looks the same. Medically too, her condition has not improved much. Apart from the broken bones, nothing inside her has healed, and nothing in me has been fixed either. I am still haunted every night and every waking moment. All I do is pray for a miracle.

Her body is functional now and she sits up with assistance. Her mother is her sole caregiver. A mother's love for her child is so pure and unconditional that no one can ever replace it. She is there for her morning and night, caring for her as if she were a newborn baby. I have apologized to her for my behaviour towards her in the past; I still do every time we meet, and all she tells me is to limit my visits now as the doctors have almost given up.

'Move on now. You need to. This is what she would want too,' her mom tells me every time I have my Sunday morning breakfast with her, at her home. I know that secretly she doesn't want me to move on, just as I do not wish to forget the past and start afresh. She too believes that a miracle might happen some day, and that day Adira would want me to be with her; and I would be there, no matter what anyone tells me. Her mother greets me at the doorstep every Saturday with the hope that one day, her daughter will react to my presence there; one day she will respond to my love for her.

Adira was discharged from the hospital after a month-long stay. The doctors said that the swelling in her brain had gone down considerably, and yet they could not find out why she was not reacting to anything. Her stats were that of a healthy individual, her injuries had healed, but her condition remains the same. During her last days at the hospital, she had started sitting with support as she was lifted up from her bed by the hospital staff. However, she was force-fed liquid food, and her facial expressions never changed; they still don't. She keeps on staring at something far away, with her hollow eyes which have no hope, joy or sorrow in them. Earlier, her eyes were pushed open by the staff or her mother every morning. What has changed since she came back home is that she now opens her eyes on her own in the morning, indicating that she is awake, and closes them at night. We know that she is there with us, but she does not realize or acknowledge our presence.

My parents and sister had come back to Delhi and got to know about Adira's accident while she was still in the hospital. They came there to meet her. They saw her, and they also saw me being there for her but said nothing. No one brought her topic up in our house. I had confined myself to my room whenever I was at home. I left work to be with her during the morning hours, and locked myself up in my room in the evenings. I skipped meals to reach the hospital on time and help her mother who wanted to take care of her all alone. But none of my efforts matter now, for I did not do what I should have done when I could.

The day she was finally discharged from the hospital, her mother proposed that we visit my house once, for it might trigger something in her; the memories might bring her back. I told my parents who were as helpful and understanding as any parents could be. I had not been communicating with them. I never allowed anyone to enter my room, not even the maid for cleaning. I had printed out all the pictures of her that I had ever clicked and framed them, in delicate golden frames; for golden is her favourite colour and suited her best. They were all over the room, occupying every inch of the now-barren walls, and I wanted no one to disturb them.

When Adira was wheeled into the room, I hoped she would remember something. I looked at her eyes, for I believed that I had seen them respond, no matter what the doctors told us. I had seen them twinkle when I sang '*Chod do anchal . . .*' for her in the hospital, and I saw her pupils dilate every time I told her how much I loved her. Her mother too vouched that she had seen her daughter's eyes dilate at times, but the doctors dismissed our claims and told us that it was all in our head.

'This is common. The loved ones feel and see movements even when there aren't any. Your mind is trying to trick you,' we were told every time. That day, when we took her into the room, I saw nothing in her eyes. Her soulful eyes had become hollow and empty, and I cannot forget the look in them.

Her mother took all her pictures with her. She also made me promise that I will not fill the room with her photographs any more, for she thinks that I do not deserve all the pain that I am going through. How can I tell her that I deserve that and a lot more? She is wrong in thinking that not looking at her pictures will help me move on.

I shall wait for her all my life if I have to.

When I last visited her, I told her that I was writing a book about us, about our love story. She did not react to my words, but I know that one day, she will be reading this book, lying next to me on the bed, by the light of a table lamp with her reading glasses on.

This book is for you, Adira.

For a long time, I have not been able to find myself, for I am still lost in you.

ACKNOWLEDGEMENTS

The world is a better place because of people who help others achieve their dreams. I want to thank Ravinder Singh for being my mentor and guide throughout the journey. His words have inspired me and my writing.

A special thanks to my editor, Vaishali Mathur, and her entire team at Penguin Random House for their editorial help.

Finally, a big thank you to all my readers who motivate me to complete my stories.